Can I Tell You Something?

Holly June Smith

D1492827

Contents

For all the friends I've loved in the mountains

A Note From Holly

Thank you for reading *Can I Tell You Something?* I hope you enjoy it as much as I enjoyed writing it.

Please be advised that this book is an open-door romance featuring on-page sexual content for mature readers only.

There are several audio extracts throughout this book which feature [TAGS]. If you're unfamiliar with the audio erotica world, think of these as tropes. A way for listeners to quickly get a sense of the content.

This is a fun, cosy (and spicy!) Christmas novella with low angst. However, there are brief mentions of cheating (previous partners), and mental health and panic attacks (in the past). If these are challenging for you, please take care.

About the Author

Holly June Smith is a writer and romance addict who is constantly falling in love with fictional heroes and dreaming up new ones.

Holly is also a wedding celebrant who helps couples celebrate their beautiful real-life love stories.

Originally from the North East of Scotland, she now lives in Hertfordshire, England, with her partner, their two children, and a TBR that threatens to crush her in her sleep.

You can find her online @hollyjunesmith

Chapter 1
Hannah

FOR AS LONG AS I can remember, Christmas has always meant three things: snow, skiing, and sugar cookies.

Ever since I was a baby, my family has spent Christmas and New Year at my grandma's chalet in the French Alps. The first thing we'd do when we arrived in the sleepy mountain village was head straight to the *patisserie* for cookies. And since my brother, Ryan, isn't joining us this year, *again*, that means I'll get to eat them all by myself.

At least, that's the positive spin I'm putting on spending Christmas alone with my parents.

I could stay in London, but the thought of waking up in my poky little flat alone on Christmas morning is too depressing. My grandma is sadly no longer with us, and though Dad suggested I bring a friend, I've been working so hard I haven't been keeping up with my social circle much. Plus, it's always been *our place*. I wouldn't love it so much if I were hyper analysing our annual traditions through the eyes of an interloper.

Truthfully, I need this trip, and I need a break. My first year as a lawyer has been intense, and I feel guilty about taking time off. The workload will only get heavier, so I don't know if I'll be able to visit the mountains again after this year. Ryan certainly finds it difficult now that he's working out in L.A.

My brother moved to California for film school a few years ago, and now he's working hard to make a name for himself in TV production. In fact, he's working so hard he didn't make it home last year, nor the year before that, and he's not making this one either. Which means I haven't seen my brother in three years, and... ugh. I swallow hard and fix a smile on my face as I inch along in the queue.

I know that's what's really getting me down, but I can't push the thought away. A lifetime of Christmases in the happiest place in the world will soon become a distant memory. No more competing for top speed, no stuffing ourselves with fondue, and no sledging home from dinner in the dark.

It's the end of an era, another thing outside of my control. Much like the dark clouds threatening to delay my flight.

London City airport is packed with businessmen frantically typing and aggressively shouting into their phones as they shuffle their way through long security lines. I swear this is the most testosterone filled airport in the country, and every briefcase owner in London is escaping for winter break.

I briefly wonder where all their luggage is, before remembering I'm amongst the one percent here. Men who aren't quite wealthy enough to justify a private jet, but likely have holiday homes stocked with every outfit they could possibly need, including the latest winter sports gear. And a driver to collect them once we land in Geneva, of course.

I can hardly judge them. I am off to my family's chalet after all, but ours is small by Alpine standards. My ski gear lives there all year round, but I've still had to cram everything I need into my cabin sized bag, lest I get stiffed for fees on both legs of the journey. Fortunately, it's mostly comfy loungewear and I'll enjoy a visit to a French pharmacy to stock up on toiletries and skincare.

After collecting my hand luggage from security, thankfully without being stopped for an extra bag check, I weave my way through the Duty Free shop.

I'm tempted by a giant Toblerone. We used to beg Dad to buy them for us, but he always refused and told us the artisanal, handmade chocolates we could buy in the mountains would be worth the wait. He wasn't wrong, and I've been a snob about chocolate ever since, but those chunky triangles still have a certain allure.

Gin, however, that I certainly will need if I'm to survive two weeks alone with parents who will only want to talk about my career plans and lack of relationship status. I can hardly wait to be ambushed before I've even taken off my coat. I pay for two bottles of Malfy and scroll Instagram as I weave through the crowds.

The departures board has no gate listed, so I'm early enough for a glass of champagne and a spot of people watching. After ordering, I nab a high stool along the bar that faces out towards the crowds and settle in.

Several extremely attractive men stroll by. There are those in suits and tailored wool coats, others in dark jeans that hug them in all the right places, shirt buttons open at the collar just so. Some are alone, others are in a group, frenetic chatter that suggests they're also about to kick back and enjoy some downtime together. One man catches my eye as he walks towards me, a dazzling smile spread across his clean-shaven face.

A girl could do well for herself in a place like this. A girl with confidence and charisma, that is. I'm cursed to flush beetroot red and look down at my feet until he passes me by.

My dating life is abysmal, and that's nobody's fault but my own. I've dabbled with apps, and agreed to being set up a few times, but no man can scratch my particular itch.

The truth is, I have deep-rooted trust issues. That and I'm already in all-consuming love with a man who lives on the other side of the world, has no idea I exist, and makes me come multiple times a night.

And if I want him, as I often do, all I have to do is push in my earbuds, and there he is, ready to whisper the most delicious filth straight into my ears.

You see, the man of my dreams is American audio erotica voice actor, *Mac'n'Please.*

In my search for sexual stimulation a little less aggressive than mainstream pornography, I found audio porn on Reddit a couple of years ago. Entire libraries of creators work featuring every fantasy you could ever think of, plus plenty I could never have come up with on my own. There are sexy stories, creator confessions, guided masturbation tutorials, and even comfort audios to soothe you into a blissful sleep. I can't tell you exactly what drew me to Mac, except that after two minutes of listening to his voice, I was more turned on than I'd ever been with any man in real life.

I've been shamefully addicted ever since. Not that seeking sexual gratification is anything to be ashamed of, but it's not the sort of thing you bring up at parties. Though at this point, I'd rather spend my evenings at home listening to men moaning than pretending to be confident enough for parties.

Me: Just boarded

Ryan: Safe travels

My brother's blunt replies are a new thing, mostly caused by a heavy workload. When we both lived at home our parents couldn't shut us up. Now, I'm half convinced I'd never hear from him if I didn't force him to call me and check in once a week.

Me: Sure I can't change your mind?

Ryan: Afraid not. Work is crazy busy right now

Me: More chocolate for me then

The first Christmas he missed, I was seriously pissed off, but I can't be mad when I know he's working so hard at a job that he loves.

My seatbelt securely in place, I impatiently watch the safety briefing. The second it's over, I connect my bluetooth headphones, find my favourite *Mac'n'Please* audio, and hit play.

Mac 'n' Please

Bumping into your Ex

[M4F] [Exes to Lovers] [Reminiscing] [Emotional] [Kissing] [I Remember Everything] [Soft Dom] [Consent] [Fingering] [Oral] [Finish Inside] [Communication]

Holy shit. I can't believe you're here. It's been, what, five years? How have you been?

I'm really glad to hear that. You look well.

Yeah, really good actually.

No, not better than I remember. Just as good. You were always gorgeous.

*Yeah, I'm good. Teaching fourth grade now, so that's...
loud. But they keep me on my toes. I love it and they love
me. They call me Mister Mac and think I'm the coolest
guy on the planet.*

The moms? (laugh)

*Is that your subtle way of asking if I'm dating anyone?
Because you're not subtle.*

No. I'm not dating anyone. Are you?

Chapter 2
Cameron

I'M WAY TOO BUZZED to be on a plane, and we haven't even taken off yet.

In my defence, had I known I'd be flying tonight I wouldn't have gone for drinks after work, but if I hadn't had so much to drink chances are we wouldn't be flying at all.

"Would you gentlemen like something from the bar?" the flight attendant asks, her pretty smile painted with pink lipstick. A story writes itself in my mind. Seducing someone on a plane and hooking up in the cramped bathroom. Or maybe making a fellow passenger come with my fingers hidden underneath a blanket on a night flight with the lights dipped low. I bet my listeners would be into that one.

"Two rum and Cokes, please," Ryan asks, but I lean across him and hold up my hand.

"No rum for me, thank you. Just the Coke." Ryan gives me that look, the one that says I'm being a buzzkill. "Dude, this is a fifteen hour trip, and I already feel hammered."

"So have one more, then pass out. You'll wake up fresh as a daisy."

He's full of shit. We have a layover in London before the second leg of our journey. Sleep is not on the cards. France is nine hours ahead, and I don't know how I'll cope with jetlag. Basically, I'm fucked whether I drink more or not.

posted a few recordings on Reddit, built up a fanbase, then set up my subscription only site for exclusive content.

To put it bluntly, twice a week I set up my microphone, take off my pants, tell dirty stories, and jerk off. And it turns out there are many people willing to pay for the pleasure of listening to me moan.

Of course, there's more to it than that. There's scripting, editing, not to mention foley work. These audios only sound genuine when the background noise adds to the story, but thankfully my day job has given me plenty of insight into what works. Sometimes I take on scripted work for a couple of writers I know, but mostly it's just me and my hand doing the hard work, so to speak.

Our attendant friend reappears on the other side of the aisle, crouching by my side with her hand resting gently on my armrest. "Before we take off, are you sure you have everything you need, sir?"

"We're all good, thank you."

"Well, if you need anything, absolutely anything you need, you just—"

"We'll buzz," I nod. "Of course. Thank you."

When she's out of earshot, Ryan laughs from behind his fist, then leans over to punch me in the arm. "Dude, she definitely recognises you."

Oh God, not this again.

Three women recognised me in a bar a few months ago, and Ryan hasn't let me live it down since.

"She wants you," he whispers, taunting me.

"No, she doesn't. She's probably trying to figure out if we're anyone worth knowing."

The great thing about audio porn is that it can be enjoyed by anyone, anywhere, at any time. It's inclusive, non-judgemental, there's truly something for everyone. Based on comments my listeners leave,

I know there are women, and men, of all ages and all backgrounds, listening all over the world. So yeah, there's every chance she might recognise me, but even if she did, I wouldn't do anything about it.

Mac is a character, a role I play. Sure, he's also me and my body and my words, but the lines get blurred. On the few occasions I've met a listener, they've made assumptions about me based on what they've heard. And any dates I've told have found the whole thing either a confusing turn-off or wanted to record together, which is not something I'm keen to do.

Those women in the bar treated me like a conquest, a prize to be won. I mean, I know that's what women have to deal with on a regular basis, but that doesn't make it right.

"I bet she follows your Insta. Look," he giggles drunkenly, pointing up to where she's standing in the galley looking at an iPad. "She's looking you up right now."

"You're ridiculous."

But fuck, maybe she does recognise me.

My account grew a lot this year after a few of my audios went viral on booktok. Most voice actors choose to stay anonymous, but I had nothing to lose by showing my face. To be honest, it's an easy way to promote my work that doesn't require hours of making graphics and videos.

"Well, either way, she wants you."

I fish my headphones and sleep mask out of my bag. "Shut up and finish your rum."

Chapter 3

Hannah

THIS IS THE LIFE. My happy place.

Stretched out on the chaise longue in front of floor to ceiling windows, my body wrapped in cosy plaid pyjamas and fluffy socks, underneath an old quilt my Grandma made before I was born.

This is my favourite part of the house, my little quiet corner where I can keep to myself, but still be near the action.

Our chalet is split across three floors. The ground level is mostly taken up by the garage, but also houses a boot room, storage, and a small sauna. The stairs to the middle floor open up into the living area with a decent sized kitchen to the left, and a long dining table in front of the wall of windows that lead to the balcony. Outside are a few sun loungers where we get to enjoy the best view in the world.

The far wall is taken up by a huge stone fireplace surrounded by a comfy sofa and armchairs. In the corner are stairs leading to four bedrooms, one with an en-suite, and the others sharing a bathroom at the other end of the hall.

I showered when I got here, pulled my hair up into a bun, and slathered my favourite rescue mask over my face. In the kitchen, Dad is prepping dinner and listening to jazz, while Mum turns to a prune in the hot tub down on ground level.

Outside the window, snow is blanketing everything in white, but in here the fire is roaring. I have a large glass of red wine, my half-eaten box of sugar cookies, and a new romance novel to crack into. And most importantly, no work for two weeks.

It simply cannot get better than this.

"Shall I bring you a cheese plate, Hannah?" Dad calls from the kitchen door.

OK, I guess it can get better.

"Yes, please." I stretch a little more, loosening into myself. It's good to be back.

Dad appears a few minutes later and I sit up to receive his offering; cheese, olives, cured meats, fresh bread. He perches at the end of the chaise.

"Need a top up?"

"I'm good, thanks."

"What are you reading?" He reaches out to where I've rested it on my lap but I grab it first and tuck it down by my side.

"Oh, just some chick lit rubbish I picked up at the airport." I wince at the lie. For one, there's nothing wrong with chick lit, even if the label is outdated and derogatory. And secondly, the book I'm hiding is at the steamier end of the romance scale, a college romance about a basketball player and his coach's daughter. So far, so filthy, just the way I like it. But my dad doesn't need to know that.

"Well, I'm glad to see you taking a break, kiddo. I know how hard you've been working, but you need to remember play is important too. You think you'll be OK just hanging out with us oldies this Christmas?"

"Of course," I say, popping an olive in my mouth. "What about you, do you think you'll have time for a proper break this year?"

Dad is a workaholic, and though he's here with us physically, mentally he's terrible at switching off. He owns the media and entertainment law firm I work for, and closely oversees our booming client list. I've seen him negotiate contracts on a chairlift, and dictate legal responses over the phone from a slopeside bar during après ski.

It's been this way for as long as I can remember. Dad works and Mum socialises, but they're happy and healthy and that's all that matters.

"I've told the office I'm truly off grid this year, so barring any clients getting themselves into a mess, me and Mum are all yours. I know you're missing your brother, but that doesn't mean the three of us can't have fun. Race to the bottom of the Grizzly run in the morning? Loser buys the *chocolat chaud*."

"That sounds great," I say, knowing full well he'll let me win.

"OK, kiddo. I'll let you get back to your book. Carbonara for dinner in a bit."

Seriously, it cannot get better than this.

Mac'n'Please

Laundry Day

TAGS: [M4F] [NEIGHBOURS TO LOVERS] [Flirting] [Banter]
[In Public] [Switch] [MSub to MDom] [Oral Sex] [Consent]
[Praise] [Back to Mine]

Oh hey, it's good to see you again.

*Yeah, I know it's a huge load. I'll probably be here all
day, but I've been working so hard lately I'm really
behind on life admin.*

*I work at a tech company that's about to go public, so it's
all work and no play, unfortunately.*

*What do I do to blow off steam? Nothing really. Just
keep going and hope I don't burn out too hard.*

Chapter 4

Hannah

THE UNMISTAKABLE SOUND OF my brother bursting into the living room jolts me from my sleep.

"Surprise!"

He's here. He's really here.

I toss aside my book and my blanket as I leap up to greet him.

"What are you doing here?" I wrap my arms around him and the scruff of his beard tickles my face. It's a recent development, one I've only seen online, and it will take some getting used to. Ryan might be older than me by two years, but he's always been my idiot brother, goofing around and never missing an opportunity to make things a competition between us.

"What's going on?" Dad appears from the kitchen, wiping his hands on a towel.

"Hey, Dad," Ryan smiles.

"My boy," he says, crossing the room and pulling him into a bear hug. "My boy! I can't believe it. Oh, this is the best Christmas present ever. And who's this?"

I'd been so shocked, so focused on Ryan, that I had paid no attention to the other man standing behind him. The tall man with a mop of dark waves, a strong jaw, and a little scar in his eyebrow I know is from that one summer in high-school where he wore a piercing.

No.

It can't be.

"This is my best bud and roommate, Cameron," he says, stepping back to slap him on the back and bring him into the fold. "He can't ski for shit, but he's going to spend winter break with us. I hope that's OK? We wanted to surprise you. Cam, this is my dad, Mark, and my sister, Hannah."

Cameron?

It can't be, but it is.

I'd know that face anywhere. The furrow in his brow. The wide, natural smile that's 80% boyish charm, and 20% *'I'm going to ruin you.'* The full lips I've imagined kissing me a thousand times.

"Good to meet you, sir," Cameron says, shaking Dad's hand with both of his. "Nice to meet you, Hannah."

I'm frozen to the spot. All I can do is raise my hand in a half wave and make a weird, high-pitched grunting noise that sounds nothing like *'hello'.*

"Of course it's OK. Welcome!" Dad cheers, the conversation continuing in a haze around me. "The more the merrier. I can't believe you're here. Your mother will have a fit."

He walks to the bottom of the wooden staircase. "Cheryl, you'll want to see this," he yells up.

"What's all the commotion?" she says, descending gracefully.

"Look who's here," Dad beams, and she skips down the last steps.

"Oh my God, Ryan. You could have warned me we have company. I'm practically indecent," she shrieks, pulling her silk robe tighter around her as she rushes towards him. There's her version of indecent, which is glamorous even once she's removed her make-up, and then there's my version. I look down at myself, scruffy pyjamas hanging all askew. My hair is a mess, and I bet my lips are stained with red wine.

"I'll be right back," I say, bolting to take the stairs to my room two at a time.

This can't be happening.

It can't be possible that my brother is home for Christmas, and of all the people he'd bring with him, he's brought the man I've spent over a year fantasising about.

Audio erotica voice actor *Mac'n'Please* is in my house.

Maybe he has a twin. A doppelgänger. Maybe I'm hallucinating. It's the wine and cheese.

I grab my phone and pull up his Instagram stories to see if he's posted anything since I last checked. Sure enough, there he is. A selfie on the plane, in the same black Vans hoodie as the one he's wearing downstairs in my living room. *'The mountains are calling and I must go'* written over the top in his preferred aesthetic font.

He's actually here.

For winter break. Which is two weeks long. I am doomed.

Within a month of finding his Reddit account, I'd listened to everything he'd posted, and I've been refreshing his page daily ever since.

Like a schoolgirl with a crush, I soon found his Instagram, where he posts pictures of food, dogs he meets, sunsets, and clues about his next recordings that I never get bored of trying to solve. From there it was an easy slide to subscribing to his website, where he posts exclusive audios, his direct to listener series, and tasteful photos that aren't naked enough for my liking. But his Instagram stories are my favourite place he shows up online.

Sometimes he livestreams from his bed first thing in the morning. I'll be heading home from class, and I can watch along, imagining his words are only for me, wishing I was there in his warm sheets, my face pressed to his chest. I just know he smells so good.

Sometimes he doesn't post all weekend and I wonder if there's a girlfriend, someone keeping him busy, but I don't let myself think about it for too long because in my head, Mac is mine.

I know I'm ridiculous. I know I'm being presented with a persona, but there is something so comforting about his content, about listening to him describe the way he wants to touch me, his listeners.

Don't judge me. After a long day at work there's nothing better than a self administered O and falling asleep basking in the afterglow with a man who'll never leave you, hurt you, or do you wrong. Why would you bother with a real man when you could have an audio one talk you through pretty much any fantasy scenario you can think of?

Want to get frisky with your co-worker in the copy room? He has an audio for that.

Always fancied a friends-to-lovers hook-up on a pile of coats at a party? He has an audio for that too.

Got a fantasy about one last hate-fuck with your toxic ex? Well no, not personally, but when Mac plays the role, then yes, I most certainly do.

The closest thing I can compare it to is someone ringing me for top tier phone sex, calling me a good girl, and then shushing me to sleep. It's practically a meditation exercise at this point.

I'm not deluded, except I am a little bit deluded because I want him so much. Not just for his words, but his brain, too. The way he laughs, his little jokes. He's a smart guy, curious about the world and people, with a *joie de vivre* I am personally lacking.

I've spent countless hours zoning out and daydreaming about him. I listen to his Spotify playlists, for fuck's sake. I wonder what it would be like to go to a party that he also attends. Would we make eyes at each other across the room? Find ourselves on adjacent seats in a quiet spot in a garden?

Never in a million years did I imagine I'd actually meet the man. Mere hours ago I was listening to the sound of him moaning in my ear as he played the part of a hot DILF next door who'd popped round to fix my shower and drag me underneath the water with him.

"Hannah, dinner's ready," Dad calls up the stairs. I tug my hair loose, fluff it in the mirror, change into actual clothes, then scramble through my make-up bag for a touch of mascara.

Everyone is seated at the dinner table when I make it downstairs. It's a huge rustic piece that's been in the chalet for as long as I can remember, surrounded by locally made wooden chairs with traditional alpine hearts carved into the backs. It seats ten, but with only five of us here, Dad has set the places at one end, giving Cameron the prized spot at the head of the table, on my left.

"So tell us about you Cameron, what do you do?" Dad asks once we've all loaded our plates with steaming piles of carbonara.

"I'm a sound tech at the same studio as Ryan, and I do some voice acting on the side." I nearly choke on my water.

"Wow," Mum says, clearly impressed. "What sort of shows do you work on?"

"Right now I'm working on a Netflix adaptation, but I don't think I can say any more than that." He holds his hands up and shakes his head.

"And would we have heard your voice on anything?"

Mac, sorry, *Cameron,* shifts uncomfortably in his chair and clears his throat. I stare into the middle of the table, certain my cheeks have turned into two bright red cartoon circles. Surely he's not about to admit to what he does *to my parents.*

"I'm not sure about that. A couple of commercials, nothing special."

I want to scream, but I manage to catch it before it becomes anything bigger than a small yelp. *'Nothing special'* is the polar opposite of the magic this man can work with his voice. When I realise everyone is staring at me, I focus on my plate and twist another forkful into my mouth.

"Well, it sounds fascinating," Mum continues.

"You got a good contract lawyer?" Classic Dad, never off duty. "That's my line of work."

"I do. I'm very happy with him."

"You never can be sure who to trust with these things. Be sure to reach out if you need a second pass on anything."

"Thank you, sir." God, he's so bloody charming, and polite. How is he just sitting there at our dining table, raking his fingers through his hair, existing in my world. I know what he looks like underneath his clothes and it's all I can think about.

I'm zoning out when I feel a sharp kick to the shins underneath the table.

"Why are you so quiet?" Ryan asks.

"Just listening," I shrug, grabbing another piece of garlic bread before he can pry any further.

"Will you join us for some skiing on this trip?" Mum says.

"I'm hoping to, ma'am, but I've never been before. I'm more of a beach boy, but Ryan assured me there's no better place to learn than the Alps."

"Hannah will give you some lessons. She's an excellent teacher."

"Er..." I stumble for an excuse. I can't possibly be expected to spend any time alone with this man and keep my wits about me. "I'm not very good."

"Hannah, be serious," Mum scolds. "She's an incredible skier and has taught many of our friends over the years. She'll take you up to the beginner slopes tomorrow."

"And I have plenty of kit you can borrow downstairs," says Ryan.

"That would be great," he says, turning that smile on me. "Though I have a little work to do while I'm here, so I might skip out on a day or two if it's OK to have some alone time here in the house?"

"Of course," Dad says. "Anything exciting?"

"Just want to get ahead of things for the new year. Nothing too taxing, shouldn't take long."

"Good man, I like that work ethic."

Surely he's not going to do *that* kind of audio work here? My thighs press together at the thought of him speaking his filthy words in this very house. The visual of him sitting on the chaise, my favourite spot, with his hand in his underwear, floods my mind. I squeak, then cover it by clearing my throat.

"So, Hannah," Cameron says, leaning closer. "What time do you want me?"

If I wasn't so on edge, I'd be picking my jaw up off the floor. "Huh?" is all I manage.

"Tomorrow morning. For my lesson." His smile is beautiful and deadly. I'm going to die on this trip. I won't survive looking at his gorgeous face every day, hearing that caramel voice, laughing across the table.

"Um, we usually head up after breakfast. Say, 9:30?"

"Sounds perfect. I'm looking forward to it."

I don't know what switch flipped, what threw the earth off its axis, what I've done to deserve this karma. All I know is that I'm teaching the man who's made me come more times than I can count to ski in the morning, and he has no idea who I am.

Mac 'n' Please

At the Bar

Tags: [M4F] [Strangers to Lovers] [MSub] [Begging] [Grinding] [Riding] [Eye Contact] [Multiple Orgasms] [Round 2]

Excuse me, sorry. Can you show me your tattoo? Sorry, I've been trying to get a closer look, but I don't want to come off like a creep.

Wow, it's beautiful. You have great style. I'm Mac. What's your name?

Pretty.

Are you here with friends or... someone?

Do you want to get out of here?

Chapter 5

Cameron

RYAN SERIOUSLY DOWNPLAYED HIS sister. I mean sure, it would have been weird as fuck if he said *'Yeah she's gorgeous, knock yourself out'*, but he could have warned me. Gorgeous doesn't even begin to describe her. She's breathtaking.

The vision of her when we first arrived is seared into my brain. Messy bun, a pink crease in her cheek from where she'd been sleeping, her top slipped off her shoulder just enough to expose her collarbone. Light brown eyes with long lashes, and her huge, bright smile that, unfortunately for me, was meant for her brother.

She didn't even notice me until their dad said hi.

At dinner, she barely spoke and refused to look my way, no matter how hard I tried to catch her eye. She's probably pissed off that I've gatecrashed her family holiday and now she has to spend it with a stranger instead of relaxing.

"You boys need another beer?" Ryan's mum calls down from the balcony to where he, his dad and I are chilling in the hot tub.

Mark drains his bottle. "I could go for one more."

"Me too," Ryan says.

"I'm all good. Thanks Mrs Richmond."

"Please Cameron, call me Cheryl."

"Will do, Cheryl," I say, tipping my bottle her way.

It's beautiful here, sitting in the warm water, surrounded by pure white snow under a sky full of stars. Part of me wished Hannah would come and join us, but the other part is grateful I don't have to see that woman in a swimsuit right now. Especially not when I'm sitting next to her father.

After dinner, she disappeared to her room while Ryan showed me around the house, and to the room where I'm staying. Right next to hers.

She'll be in there, in her bed, right on the other side of the wall. I was joking when I said I'd be trapped for two weeks with a woman I couldn't touch, but now that's increasingly looking like my reality.

I yawn loudly as the beer buzz takes hold.

"I think I need to take a shower and hit the hay if I'm expected to learn to ski tomorrow. I barely slept on the flight."

"OK man, see you in the morning."

"Goodnight, Cameron," Mr Richmond says. "Good to have you with us, son."

I climb out, grab my towel, and duck inside. The layout of this place is weird, and I need to walk upstairs, through the living room, then up another flight to the bathroom next to my room. With any other family, it would probably be awkward, but I'm already feeling pretty at home with everyone. Everyone except Hannah, the enigma.

"Oh dear God," she says, almost bumping into me as she rounds the bottom of the stairs with her nose buried in a book. "Sorry, I didn't see you there. I just came to get a glass of water."

I don't miss the way her eyes trace over my chest, down to my abs, before coming to a stop on the towel around my waist.

"Can't blame you," I say, tapping the front cover. "I've heard great things about that series. Horny cowboys, right?"

"Right," she says, plastering her back to the wall as she steps around me.

In my line of work, it's good business to keep up with what's popular in the literary world. There's a lot of crossover between romance novels and audio erotica, and some of my most popular audios were inspired by best-selling books.

I get a good look at her when she walks to the kitchen, her pert ass and short shorts drawing my gaze before she rounds the corner. She has the kind of thighs you want to use for a pillow. Eyes you want to get lost in, soft dark hair that looks perfect for stroking while you hold her tight.

What the fuck is wrong with me?

It's gonna be a long two weeks. Yesterday I was sitting in a bar, now I'm in a cosy little cabin in the mountains where I'm supposed to try to sleep in the room next to a beautiful woman while my brain is running wild with thoughts of her naked under my red checked blanket. Or was that two days ago? Is this jetlag-induced hallucinations? It's been a while since I hooked up with anyone. Maybe this is my brain playing tricks on me. She's just a woman, one who doesn't even seem to like me. I can certainly keep my dick in check.

Ryan talks about his family plenty, but I've never seen photos of him and his sister. I bet with a little sleuthing I can find her online and learn a few things that will get me into her good books. What she's like, what she's into, whether we have any common ground.

I start in the obvious place, Ryan's Instagram account. His social media is purely for work purposes, unlike mine, which I use to promote my *Mac'n'Please* audio work and grow my listener base. He doesn't even follow me, the prick. Said he didn't want to be associated with such filth. I should remind him that said filth paid for our asses to fly here business class.

I scroll through his followers list, and there she is. Hannah Richmond, with a public profile.

Jackpot.

If I was feeling a little more bold, I'd hit follow. Except... that button doesn't say *'follow'*. It says *'follow back'*.

Then it hits me, the knot I already had in my stomach twisting tighter. My best friend may not follow my audio erotica voice acting account, but his sister does.

Chapter 6
Hannah

THIS IS THE LEAST relaxed I have ever felt in my life. Normally if I can't sleep I stick my earbuds in and let Mac tell me exactly how to get myself off until I wear myself out, but how can I do that when he's right on the other side of the wall?

I came here hoping for two weeks of eating, drinking, skiing, and sleeping. Now my heart is pounding so hard I'm sure he'll hear it through the wood. I'll certainly never be able to sleep.

Cameron kept this side of his work close to his chest over dinner, but what if I accidentally let slip that I know who he is and what he does? I've listened to this man come so many times it's rewired my brain. He could talk to me about sinkholes and drainage systems and I'd probably get turned on. He just has to breathe and I'm a mess.

How did I miss this?

I know he lives in L.A., and so does my brother, but L.A. is massive. Assuming everyone knows everyone is like assuming every Scottish person is related, or that I can recite every law off by heart.

This is all Ryan's fault. He only uses social media to post about shows he's been working on. Why couldn't he be a normal fuckboy who posts pictures from parties like everyone else our age? I could have harnessed the power of social media and figured out his roommate's identity ages ago.

Not that it would have mattered. The man is already an addiction I couldn't quit, even if I wanted to. I'm practically a stalker, checking his accounts morning and night for new content, listening to audios the second something new drops, sending him my...

Oh God.

Oh, fuck no.

I have been known, on occasion, after a couple of drinks, and more than a few orgasms, to DM *Mac'n'Please*. He never reads them, and I've always been OK with that, but it's the only way I could express how much I appreciate his work.

What if he finds me on Instagram and sees everything I've sent him? The thought is like a bucket of ice cold water being tipped over my head.

Frantic, I grab my phone from my bedside, open Instagram, navigate to his profile and click into our message history. It's an embarrassingly one-sided conversation that goes back months and months. I scramble to delete everything,—*how the fuck do you delete DMs?*—then I watch in horror as a four letter word appears at the bottom of my screen.

Seen.

Chapter 7

Cameron

HOLY SHIT.

> *"This was one of your best yet, thank you so much. You sounded pretty exhausted by the end of it. I hope you had a great sleep and have relaxing weekend plans."*

> *"You really poured your heart into this one and it shows. I don't know how you do it, but you always say the exact thing I need to hear in the moment. You have a gift."*

> *"I never come harder than when listening to your voice."*

Those barely scratch the surface of the messages she's sent me. I keep scrolling, reading everything she's sent me over the past year or more. Some are kind and full of praise, others are filthy as fuck.

She's not pissed at me, she's in shock. She would never in a million years have imagined I'd turn up here at her house.

I now know three things. Hannah knows exactly who I am. She's got a dirty, dirty mouth. And my one rule is about to be pushed to the limit.

Mac 'n' Please

Rule Breaker

TAGS: [M4F] [HUSBAND] [MDOM] [Possessive] [Brat] [Degradation] [Spanking] [Orgasm Control] [Denial] [Mine] [Rough] [Aftercare]

Tsk, tsk, tsk. What do we have here?

No, don't try to hide it. I caught you red-handed.

What did I tell you, baby? I said, hands off until I came home from my work trip.

So what I need to know is how many times did you make yourself come while I was away?

(Growl)

Seven? So even though you knew you shouldn't, you kept going, and you kept count? You little brat.

Don't give me that look.

We made a deal, sweetheart. You broke my one rule. Now bend over my knee and take your punishment.

Chapter 8

Hannah

RYAN AND CAMERON ARE already at the dining table when I make it down for breakfast. My night of terrible sleep shows. I've attempted to make myself presentable with a bit of light make-up and the neat braids I style for underneath my ski helmet, but I still feel like a mess.

Cameron knows I know who he is.

Not only that, he knows I've listened to his audios, and that I've gotten off to them. And he knows because I was dumb enough to message him directly and tell him. I want to slap past Hannah around the head. What kind of lawyer leaves a paper trail like that?

I pour coffee and make breakfast at the counter with my back to the boys. How can I happily tuck into my muesli when the man who makes me come with just his words is sitting across the table from me, and *knows I know who he is.*

Maybe a Christmas at home alone wouldn't be so bad after all. I could leave today. I should check flights.

"Morning Hannah," Cameron says, appearing at my side. My eyes snap upwards and lock with his. So beautiful. Grey green with flecks of gold. I've never seen eyes like them. He dips his head and lowers his voice. "Can I tell you something?"

My response to those five words is Pavlovian and full-bodied. I pinch my lips together just in time to catch a small squeak and turn to check nobody heard him. Those are the words he uses in his confessions series, the audios where it's just him spilling his darkest, dirtiest desires.

"Mmhmm."

"I'm really nervous about skiing." I glance at him, and there's a humility there that I haven't seen before. He rubs at the back of his hair.

"I'm sure you'll be great."

"Will you be patient with me if I suck?" His face is casual but his voice is low and slow, taunting. "Or are you a bossy teacher?"

It's far too easy to imagine him whispering those words into my ear in the middle of the night. Or seducing me in the stationery cupboard of a school where we both work. One thing becomes painfully clear. He might be nervous about learning to ski, but he's not shy about trying to catch me out.

"You'll be fine." I take my seat at the table.

"Come on, man," Ryan interrupts, getting up to toss his dishes in the sink. "Come down to the boot room with me and I'll get you kitted out."

My shoulders barely drop as they leave me to eat, and I wonder how I'm going to survive today, and the rest of our holiday, in the company of this man and his beautiful voice.

I hang back behind my brother and Cameron as we walk to the base station, ready to board the bubble lift that will carry us part way up the mountain. We've missed the First Lift crew, the obsessives who are up and queuing to ride as soon as the network of ski-lifts creaks to life each morning. Ryan and I have always been Team Last Lift, often pleading with the lift operators to let us go up just one more time as the winter sun fades and the mountain turns pinky purple.

Still, there are plenty of people around, and Ryan points out various bars and shops along the way before taking Cameron into the ticket office for their ski-passes. I already pre-loaded online, so I hang back by the giant piste map and plot an appropriate route for a total beginner.

Mum wasn't just being kind when she offered up my teaching services. After finishing my A-Levels I almost qualified as a ski instructor. My first boyfriend and I planned to take a gap year and come out here and teach for the winter, but I dropped out of our training course when I caught him with his hands up the top of one of the other students.

The gap year was cancelled, I took up the place I'd been offered at university, and thankfully haven't thought about him much since. Unfortunately, that was just the start of the tragic dating history that has led to me ignoring most of the men I meet.

Anyway, I've been far too busy fantasising about another man. One who I'm unfortunately about to spend the next ten minutes trapped in a metal box with.

When they reappear, I show Cameron how to scan his pass, and we push through the turnstiles and follow the arrows through the base station to wait our turn.

"It comes in really fast, but then it slows right down to let us board," Ryan says, reassuring Cameron, who I now realise is entirely out of his comfort zone.

Everything about skiing is weird if you haven't done it before; heavy robot boots, carrying cumbersome skis and poles, mountain safety and the skiers' code of conduct. Not to mention feeling boiling under all those layers one minute, then the drop in temperature hitting you once we're out of the sun.

The weather is different from one day to the next in this part of the Alps, but today we've gotten lucky. Fresh snow fell overnight, and now it's a sunny day. I should have reminded him about sunscreen before we left.

"What's new with you, Sis?" Ryan asks once the doors close and we trundle out of the base station on a sharp assent of the mountainside.

"Not much," I shrug, not wanting to meet his eye.

"Come on, usually I can't get you to shut up. What's going on with you?"

"I'm fine."

"Is work kicking your ass?"

"It's nothing I can't handle."

"You dating anyone?" he pries, and I roll my eyes. I definitely don't want to talk about this in front of Mac, sorry, Cameron.

Ryan and I have never kept secrets from each other, and though he knows I typically make smart choices, he's been witness to my extremely bad choices and the resulting crappy break-ups. He's protective in a way that I appreciate, a person to confide in without being overbearing. Telling him I'm not dating right now because nobody can top his best friend is clearly not an option.

"I find it hard to believe you haven't been snapped up," Cameron says, grunting as Ryan delivers an elbow to his ribs.

"Quit hitting on my sister."

"I'm not, man. I'm just saying she seems really nice." He gestures casually towards me and I stare out of the window and keep my mouth shut for the rest of the ride.

Chapter 9
Hannah

IT TURNS OUT THIS beach boy is a great student. We've spent a couple of hours taking repeated runs on a beginner slope and he's listened well, followed all my instructions, and hasn't fallen once.

Fortunately for me, he also hasn't mentioned the shitshow that went down last night. Honestly, I'm so happy to be back on my skis in these beautiful mountains, it's hard to worry about it for long.

"Are you sure you haven't done this before?"

"I swear!" he says, following my tracks as I slalom slowly from one side of the beginner run to the other.

"You're a great teacher."

"You're a natural," I call back over my shoulder. "You'll be riding double black runs before you know it."

We come to a stop at the bottom of the valley where several pistes converge at the best pizza place in the area. It's a little early for lunch, but my stomach is rumbling, clearly not used to this much exercise in the morning.

"You want to grab a crepe and have a quick break?"

"Sure," Cameron says, lifting his goggles up to the front of his helmet. His cheeks are pink, a faint line already visible at the top of them.

"You've caught the sun," I say, unable to stop staring.

"So have you," he says, but I know I slathered on factor 50 sunscreen this morning, and what he's seeing are my blushes.

We slide over to the front of the restaurant and push back our bindings to step out of our skis. I show Cameron how to clip them together and stack them carefully in the rack.

"Won't somebody steal them?" he asks.

"It's pretty rare, and we won't be far. You find a table and I'll be back in a sec."

Inside, I visit the bathroom quickly before washing my hands and fixing my sweaty helmet hair. Carefully, I climb back up the rubber-lined stairs that are wet and laden with clumps of snow from ski and snowboard boots.

At the counter, I order and pay for two crepes with chocolate and banana, and decide to double down and order hot chocolates for us both too. They make everything fast and fresh here, so I watch Cameron through the cafe windows while I wait.

Maybe stopping was a mistake. What if he uses this downtime to bring up my messages? Even the thought of him broaching the subject has my stomach churning.

He seems relaxed though, his elbows on the table as he watches other skiers make their way down the mountain. His hair is a sweaty mess from wearing his helmet all morning too, and all I want to do is run my fingers through it. In the time I've followed him online, he's always kept it this way, and while most of my fantasies are sexual, there's a sweetness I crave from him too. I wonder what it would be like if I could take my seat next to him and reach out to touch him freely.

Mac'n'Please has a few BFE audios, or Boyfriend Experience, and they're popular for good reason. Those are the ones I listen to on weekend mornings when I want to pretend I'm waking up with him.

I dream of spending the day together, curled up on the sofa reading, stopping every now and then to make out and feel each other up.

He is the master of edging and I love to imagine him teasing me all day long, building me up, and stopping every time I get close. In my dreams he'd start at breakfast, with oral on the kitchen counter, then stop right before I came and tell me it's time to go shop for groceries. In the car he'd tell me to touch myself on the drive but *'don't you dare come. If you come, I'll fuck you where everyone can see who your orgasms belong to.'*

I'd be his good girl, always doing as I'm told. Back home we'd unpack, and while preparing lunch he'd touch me constantly, but never where I need him most. We'd shower together, and he'd stroke his cock until he came in his hand, but he'd never let me touch him, and he wouldn't let me touch myself either.

In the evening, we'd go out for dinner and drinks. He'd pin me to the wall before we left the house, drop to his knees, rake his nails up underneath my skirt, and tug my underwear to the floor. He'd give me one slow lick, and my fingers would dig into his hair as my hips pushed against his face. But he'd push me back, and stand, laughing as he'd loop my damp knickers over his thumb, pull on the elastic and catapult them up the stairs.

'You won't need these,' he'd whisper, and I'd almost come on the spot.

He'd tease me all night. Fingers on my thigh. Taunts in my ear. It would be torture, but I'd love it. The anticipation, the longing, the knowledge deep down that he would fuck me eventually, but I'd have to be good and patient just a little longer.

By the time we get home, I'd be aching and soaked, practically shaking with need. Drunk on my desire to have him all over me. He'd sit on the end of our bed, make me strip for him, then lie me down and spread my legs. He'd take his time, teasing while I squirmed and begged beneath him.

And I would beg, happily, not just driven wild by lust, but because I know how much he loves to hear how desperate I am for him. When he'd finally let me come, I'd get there in seconds, but that would only encourage him. He'd never let me come once and then stop. He'd barely let me catch my breath. He'd make me count. I'd lose count. Orgasms rolling back to back, crashing through me before I'd had a second to recover from the last.

It would be one of many perfect days in our perfect life. My perfect, deluded little world.

"Deux chocolat et banane, et deux chocolat chaud," the woman behind the counter calls and I sigh, wishing I'd had a couple more seconds to daydream.

"Oui, merci beaucoup."

I carry our tray outside, grabbing cutlery from the stand by the door, and stomp my way across the wooden decking. There's no attractive way to approach a man while wearing ski boots.

"That was awesome," he says when I take the seat beside him. "But my legs are killing me."

My own legs feel like jelly, but that's nothing new around him. I kneel in front of him, tug up his ski pants, and flip open the clips on his boots.

"That should help." It's only then I realise where I've put my hand to balance myself, and the words are out before I can stop myself. "Woah, your thighs are solid."

Cameron looks back and forth between my face and my hand, somehow still dangerously high on his thigh, and now *squeezing*?

I've lost my mind.

"I work out. A lot of squats. And I used to rollerblade," he says, in a sort of trance of his own.

I finally come to my senses and pull away. "That explains it. I think skiing and skating use a lot of the same muscles, the same core balance."

"I say *'used to'*. It's been years since I've used those muscles."

"You'll be pretty sore tomorrow. Twenty minutes in the hot tub after dinner will sort you out. And we have a small sauna room under the stairs too. Not sure if Ryan showed you."

"Damn, he made out like your place was some tiny little wooden shack in the forest. You guys are fancy."

"Well, my grandma was fancy," I correct him. "We're just lucky descendants, I guess." Glancing back up the hill, I watch as an older gentleman traverses the slope with a kid who can't be more than four tucked between his legs. That was me once.

Granny taught us to ski and loved, much to Dad's disdain, taking Ryan and I off-piste, showing us her favourite spots all over the mountain. She was a risk taker, a rule breaker, and feisty to the end. I miss her terribly.

"You OK?" Cameron asks, bumping his shoulder up against mine. On the table, his arm rests barely an inch from mine. I swear I can feel my hairs standing on end, gravitating towards him.

"I'm good. Just reminiscing." I point at his food and tuck into mine. "Eat up before the chocolate turns solid."

We eat in silence, thankfully too hungry to pause between each mouthful, but talking is Cameron's whole life, and I get the feeling he's finding it hard to sit here and say nothing. I just hope he doesn't bring up last night.

"You want to tell me about your grandmother?" He dabs a dot of chocolate sauce from the corner of his mouth with a napkin.

"Maybe some other time."

"Tell me about you then." He shifts, angling his body towards me, and the forearm of dreams is out of reach.

"What do you want to know?" This is a dangerous question. He already knows far more than I would ever care to admit. I don't know why I've given him an opening to press for more details.

"Everything."

Oh fuck.

"That's a pretty broad range of subjects."

"Ok," he says, tapping his lip. "Let's start with... favourite ice-cream flavour?"

"Pistachio."

"Classy, I like it. Favourite season?"

"All of them. They each have their highlights."

"I'm down with inclusivity. Movie star crush?"

I roll my eyes, not willing to go there. I'm hardly going to tell him all movie stars lost their appeal the minute I heard his voice. "We should get back to skiing while the weather is on our side."

It's a pathetic excuse. There is not a cloud in the sky. I stand up and load our dishes onto the tray.

"Wait." Cameron grabs my wrist and pulls me back towards him. "One last question. I'm dying to know." Hours pass as I wait for him to stop staring at my mouth and ask what he is apparently so desperate to find out about me. "What do you like to listen to?"

No, no, no. Please don't be this bold.

We were doing so well. Can't we just pretend we're having a nice day on the mountain and there isn't this big unspoken secret between us?

"Well?"

"I... er..."

"Come on." His other hand comes up to wrap around my forearm and tightens ever so slightly, his fingertips pressing into me. I feel the heat even through the layers of my jacket. "What do you like to fill your ears with when you're alone at night, Hannah?"

His voice is rich, so laced with seduction that I'd sway backwards if he weren't keeping me upright. His eyes are on my mouth again, and my lips are about to form the word *'you'*, when I catch myself and pull out of his grip. "Let's go."

Mac'n'Please

Bumping into your Ex

Tea?

Of course I remember how you take it. I remember everything.

God, your perfume.

(Inhale deeply)

It brings back so many memories.

Of course good ones.

That spot behind your ear that smells like your sham-poo. I used to love kissing you there. I still remember the way you taste, too.

You know the way some couples have break-up sex. Did you ever wish we'd done that? One last time together, to say goodbye.

No? I do. I think about it all the time.

Chapter 10

Cameron

THIS WOMAN IS A closed book. A brick wall. An iron fortress.

All I want is for her to admit that she knows who I am, then maybe she wouldn't be so awkward around me. She's been shy around me all morning, and I'm not *trying* to make it awkward.

We should be able to laugh about it, acknowledge that it's a wild coincidence. If she wasn't so nervous around me, I bet we could probably have some fun together. She's so gorgeous, and since I know she's into a lot of the same stuff as me, it's pretty much impossible *not* to imagine us having a good time together.

Leading questions clearly aren't working, so I'm going to have to take a different approach. I think I might know just the way to get through to her, but I'll need a bit of time to myself to execute it.

I catch up with her by the ski rack as she's stepping into her bindings.

"You need to clip your boots back up first," she says, tapping my leg with her pole as I lay my skis out flat.

"I think I'll skip out for the afternoon. I have some work to catch up on, and I don't want to overdo it on the first day."

I don't miss the way her face flushes. I'm sure she's wondering what exactly that work will entail.

"OK," she says. "Let's ski back to the top of the first lift we took and you can ride it straight back down to the village."

"You don't trust me to make it back by myself?"

Her face breaks into a smile as she shakes her head slowly, her quiet laugh a beautiful sound that only reaches my ears. "I wouldn't feel OK sending you off alone on your very first day of skiing. I'd be a terrible teacher if I lost my only pupil."

"Fair enough. Do I need your keys for the house?"

"No, there's a keypad on the door. I'll message you the code so you don't have to memorise it."

I can't help but smile when she tugs her glove off with her teeth, unzips her jacket pocket, and pulls out her phone. Only when she opens up Instagram does she finally realise what she's just said. Her cheeks redden and her lips part as she stares, wide-eyed, at the floor. She knows she's fucked up, and accidentally given away the fact that she has a way to contact me.

"You don't have my number," I say eventually. I'll let her slip-up slide, this time. "Give me your phone."

I'm tempted to save my number under Mac just to really get under her skin, but the poor woman might spontaneously combust or burst into tears.

"There you go. Now you can reach me whenever you need me."

She reaches for her phone and her fingertips graze the underside of mine, sending a spark of... something through the back of my hand. She gasps, her eyes locking with mine, and I know she felt it too. My hand finds itself on her elbow, cupping it, pulling her gently towards me. Her palm lands on my waist, fingers curling around me, and suddenly we're the only two people on the mountain.

I want to pull her even closer, lift her chin, and drop my mouth to hers. I want to know what she tastes like, what her hair smells like, whether she would make a noise if I tugged on one of those pretty braids.

"We should go," she whispers, letting her hand fall back to her side. She stares at her phone as she taps out a message, and two seconds later, mine buzzes in my pocket.

"You lead the way."

She skis slowly for my benefit, and even if I didn't have an ulterior motive, going home seems like a wise idea. Despite being in one of the most magical places I've ever been, it's hard to enjoy it when my thighs are burning, and my feet are desperate to get out of these heavy boots.

"Are you sure you'll be OK getting back to the house?" she asks when we get to the lift station. For a woman who has tried to keep me at arm's length all morning, I half wonder if she wants me to ask her to come back with me. But I need her out of my hair if my plan is going to work.

"I'll be fine. You go meet your family and I'll see you when you get home."

"Enjoy your work," she says, waving me off.

Oh, she has no idea how much I'll enjoy this. It's very important work, indeed. The work of getting her to confess how much she wants me.

Mac'n'Please

Laundry Day

Oh fuck, what are you doing?

I didn't... that's not what I meant...

No, we can't do this.

Seriously? Right here in the basement? Anyone could walk in.

Are you sure?

OK. OK. Yeah, you can take it out.

(Sigh heavily)

Open your mouth.

Jesus, fuck. Well, aren't you a surprise?

(Bite lip and moan)

Yeah, just like that.

Look up at me.

You think you can take it all?

You look so fucking pretty on your knees like that.

Chapter 11
Hannah

W E   H A D   P L A N N E D   T O   meet up with Ryan and my parents for lunch, so after making sure Cameron gets on the correct lift home, I spend the rest of the morning cruising around on my own.

I won't allow myself to miss him. Sure, it's a little quiet without his constant chatter, but I need a break from feeling so on edge around him. Plus, I can ski further and faster on my own.

After a quick stop for pizza, the four of us catch lifts and ski together, just like old times.

"How did you meet Cameron?" I ask Ryan on our last chairlift of the day. It's an open two-seater that carries you up to the highest peak you can access without taking your skis off and hiking. Every year, Ryan and I get in a dumb contest to see who can make it back to the bottom of the village fastest. I know I have the edge since he hasn't skied in three years, and it shows.

"We were in film school at the same time. I needed a sound guy for a short I was working on, and a mutual friend put us in touch. Then we both ended up working for the same studio."

"And how did you end up living together?"

"Both our leases were up around the same time. He had a lead on a nice two-bedroom place near the studio, so it made sense. Better than us each having to find new roommates who turn out to be creeps."

That's interesting.

So either Ryan doesn't know about Cam's audio erotica work, or he does, but he doesn't find it creepy.

It's not something I've ever discussed with anyone else, but it definitely seems like the sort of work some people would be judgemental of.

"And do you like living with him?"

"Yeah, sure. You've seen the place on video calls, it's nice."

I could kick myself. I've seen their apartment on calls with Ryan, and other parts of it on Cameron's Instagram stories, but the walls are a generic light grey. How was I supposed to know they live together?

"Hello?" he says, raising his eyebrows. "What's with all the questions?"

"Nothing," I shrug. "I'm just curious about your life now. It's worlds away from mine."

"Well, if you'd take a break for five minutes and come out to visit, you'd get to see my side of the world too. Cam and I spotted Timothée Chalamet in a restaurant last week. You'd have loved it."

It's kind of funny that he assumes I'd care about spotting Timothée when in reality I'd be a puddle at the sight of Cameron, much like I was when he turned up in my bloody house without warning yesterday.

We cut our conversation short as the lift pulls into the top station. I hop off and jab my poles into the mostly untouched powder to shove past him. At the top of the piste, we get into position.

"Wait for us," I hear Dad yell from behind us.

"Oh Mark, let them go. There's no way I'm trying to keep up. We'll see you back at the house, kids."

"I'll see *you* back at the house, sucker!" Ryan yells, digging his poles in and pushing off hard.

"Not if I see you first!"

He might have a half-second head start, but I overtake him fast and leave him in the spray from my skis. It takes at least fifteen minutes to ski from here back to the village, though you can take as long as you like if you enjoy cruising around the mountain, stopping to admire the views on your way down.

Ryan can never resist turning off to ride through fresh powder at the side of the piste, and I love that too, but it's not the way to win this race. By the time I reach the bottom of the first run, pushing down through my poles to reach the next one, I'm a good minute ahead of him and I know I've won.

Still, the pressure is on. I don't dare slow as I zoom past groups of adults taking part in lessons, snowboarders hitting ramps they've built at the side of the slope.

I feel safe here. Happy. I can't mess anything up if I just look ahead, choose my line and follow it through. I know this mountain better than I know any other thing in my life. Every twist and turn, every distance marker, every flat that requires a buildup of speed to make it to the end.

I sail across the wide plateau halfway down the mountain. Past the little row of bars and restaurants where crowds are already enjoying their après-ski drinks and french fries. The smell of fat and salt and beer is a siren call after a day on the slopes, but that will have to wait for another day.

It isn't long until I'm back at the top of the lift where I dropped Cameron off earlier. Instead of taking it down, I veer left and glide past the line of trees that lead back to our chalet, then continue down towards the village. The snow is softer here, less groomed after a day of beginners and experts alike, each giving it their last push as they head home.

My heart is racing, breath coming in hard pants as I glance back up the mountain, expecting to see Ryan gaining on me, but there's no sign. The sun has already faded from this side of the hill, cold air pinching at my cheeks. I push out of my skis and hop down the bank into the snow covered back garden we won't see for another three or four months.

Chapter 12

Hannah

MY LEGS SHAKE AS I unbuckle my boots, stack them on the dryer in the boot room, and climb the stairs to the middle of the house. I find Cameron stretched out on the chaise with a book in his hand, looking criminally hot in dark sweatpants and a white fitted t-shirt. Nobody else ever sits in my favourite spot, and it's jarring to see him looking so at home there.

I'd been hoping to avoid him, at least until I changed out of my sweaty clothes, but it's impossible when you have to pass through the living area to go upstairs.

"Hey." He drops his book in his lap, his thumb tucked between pages so he doesn't lose his spot.

"Hey. Good afternoon?"

"Yup. You?"

"Yup," I nod, inching towards the stairs. "You comfy there?" What I really want to say is *'Can I come and sit in your lap and kiss your face and feel you get hard underneath me?'* but I'm not completely out of my mind.

"It's such a nice spot, isn't it? With this view and everything." He stretches out, feline and slow, but his eyes never look away from mine. He rests one arm above his head and I will myself not to look down at the sliver of skin exposed at his waist. I'm so horny for this man, there's every chance I'll drop to my knees and crawl over to lick it. "Let me finish this chapter and you can sit here."

"You're fine. I'm gonna take a bath, anyway."

"No hot tub?"

"Not for me. Ryan isn't far behind me, though. I'm sure he'll be up for it."

"What a shame," he says, lips tipping up as his eyes float down slowly to my chest. His stare is unbearable, like he's setting me on fire. I'm halfway up the stairs when he calls after me. "Hey, Hannah?"

I pause, knuckles turning white as I grip the bannister. "Mmm?"

"Can you teach me how to light the fire later? I wanted to get it going for when you all got home, but it keeps dying out. I don't know what I'm doing."

"Sure. Mum's the pyro of the family, though. She won't be long."

"OK, thanks. Enjoy your bath."

I don't know if my mind is playing tricks on me, but I'm sure he winks.

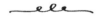

At home in London, my daily bath is something of a ritual. A regimen of oils and cleansers, masks and lotions. An hour of peace, one hand between my thighs, the breathy moans of *Mac'n'Please* in my ear. It's the only way I've found to unwind properly after solving other people's problems all day.

I don't have my usual products here, but I still run the bath deep and full of bubbles, ready to soak away the day. If I'd have had the forethought, I'd have brought a chilled glass of white wine in with me, but I'm not about to run back downstairs in a towel while Cameron reclines like some painting of a God.

With that image on my mind, I'm too tense to truly unwind anyway, fantasies coming thick and fast. Cameron comes into the bathroom and climbs into the water with me fully clothed. Or I bump into him in the hallway and he pulls at my towel until I'm standing naked before him.

After washing, I towel dry my hair, then braid it into two long plaits before heading back downstairs.

As predicted, Mum is crouched in front of the fire. Cameron kneels, attentive by her side.

"So once you've built a little tower of kindling like that, you can light the paper underneath and add a medium-sized log on top of it all. You don't want too much wood at first or it can smother the flame before it has a chance to really get going."

"That's awesome. Thank you for showing me."

Dad has a bottle of red wine breathing on the dining table, so I pour myself a glass and join them to watch the fire grow. Cameron looks up at me, face beaming, proud of his new skill. My brain pushes forth another scenario where he'd be watching me from his knees, and I back away to the sofa. It's already too hot in here.

Is this how it's going to be? Me acting like a sex-crazed maniac every time I look at him? It's impossible to play it cool.

The downstairs door opens and Ryan appears up the stairs, still in his ski pants and old hoodie.

"Are you only just back?"

"Yeah," he says, face flushed and sweaty. "Bumped into an old friend. And you were miles ahead. I had no chance of winning."

"Sounds like an excuse. Sure you didn't get lost? Run in with a tree? Wiped out by a class of five-year-olds?"

"Hilarious. I'm jumping in the shower. Hot tub in five?" he says to the rest of the room.

"Sounds good." Cameron stands, following him up the stairs, presumably to change into swim shorts. He's going to strip. Get naked. He'll be naked in his room, and even if it's just for one moment, I can't handle knowing it.

"What's for dinner, Dad?"

"Beef in an hour," he says, not looking up from the crossword puzzle he has his nose buried in at the dining table. "Want to help me finish this first?"

ele

Mum has ordered dinner in from a local catering company, a rich bœuf bourguignon with mashed potatoes and green beans that just needed to be reheated in the oven.

By the time we're done, the effects of a day's skiing are taking hold. With weary limbs and eyes that can't quite stay open, I say goodnight and take myself off to bed.

Underneath the covers, I fight a yawn as I instinctively pull up Cameron's website, knowing full well there won't be anything new.

Except there it is, right there in my hand.

NEW POST FROM MAC'N'PLEASE.

Chapter 13
Hannah

I DOUBLE CHECK MY door is closed and bluetooth connected, lie back, and press play.

Can I tell you something?

His whispers make the hairs on the back of my neck stand on end, goosebumps breaking out everywhere, knowing he's about to let me into a secret. Sure, me and every other listener, but right now I'm deluded enough to believe these words are just for me.

> *I am coming to you today from the cutest, cosiest little cabin in the French Alps. No seriously, I am. I wish I could show you, but that's kind of outside the realm of possibility in the audio world. You'll just have to take my word for it.*

Holy shit. Holy shit. Holy shit. He recorded here. In this house. While I was out. What if I'd have come back early? What if any of us came back early?

What happened is, I have this good buddy I met in film school. He's British, and it turns out his family owns a cabin - sorry, chalet - in a little ski resort high up in the mountains. Apparently, it used to belong to his grandmother, but every year they come out here for the holidays.

Now he and I were planning on kicking back over winter break, maybe hit the beach, surf, take a couple of road trips. I was gonna record a ton of these audios for you because you know when I'm bored, and I'm chilling, it just feels so natural to touch myself and pass the time that way.

I'm not embarrassed about it either. It's only natural, it's not hurting anyone. It's simply a fun activity I like to enjoy in the privacy of my own home, which I then record and put on the internet for thousands of people to hear. See? Totally normal.

He laughs then breathes deeply, exhales slowly.

But I haven't come in ages. Had a busy week at work, then travelling, and now I'm here and I'm... I'm really fucking pent up. I need to get off.

He swallows hard, and I know what's coming next.

I'm stroking it right now. Can you tell? I think you can tell. I think you can tell by the way my voice changes. You always know when I'm getting a little distracted, when I can't finish my sentences. Let me add a little more lube, and then I'll tell you how I got here.

Ohhh fuck, that feels good. That's maybe a little too much, or maybe there's no such thing when it comes to lube. I'm glad I remembered to pack some. You know I love it when it gets nice and slippery.

My brain is about to short circuit.

Where was I? Oh yeah, so my buddy was feeling kinda sad about missing his family Christmas. Obviously, Christmas in California is a completely different experience from these snowy mountains. And he's telling me about all these amazing traditions his family has, things they look forward to for months. The way he told it, it sounded like something from a Hallmark movie, you know?

Anyway, we'd had a couple of drinks after work, a good little buzz going, and I was hamming it up saying 'you should go man, be with your family', kinda jokingly pushing him out the door. But then I started looking up flights for him. And you know what we were shocked to discover? It wasn't a crazy amount to fly back. The next thing I knew, I mean... you know how this ends, right? I was hitting confirm on two business class tickets from LAX to Geneva that were leaving in three hours.

I know, I know. It was frivolous as fuck, but I'm not too proud to say I did pretty well from this website this year. From these audios that you love listening to so much. I think it's the first time in my life I could afford to do something like this without worrying about my next paycheck, so thank you, my darling, for making my little artist dreams come true.

But it was kind of funny because we were in such a rush to pack that when we rocked up to the airport in jeans and hoodies, I felt for sure we were going to get kicked off the flight. Except, it turns out most people in business were in jeans and hoodies. I guess they were all tech bros or something.

OK, hold on, I don't want to jack it to the thought of tech bros. Let me get back on track with what I really wanted to talk about.

It's kind of cute hearing about his travels from his point of view, but it's not what I want to hear about either.

Where was I? Oh, fuck, that feels good. OK, so I guess the thing I want to talk about today is the idea of Forbidden Fruit.

Long story short, me and my buddy, we arrive and hop in a transfer bus. I've never been to Europe before and I'm feeling like a motherfucking king, you know? And the drive is gorgeous, all these winding roads and snowy mountains in the distance. It took a couple of hours, but before long we're pulling up to their cabin. Sorry, chalet, fuck, I keep calling it a cabin by mistake.

I meet his mom, I meet his dad, they're super nice, salt of the earth people. I immediately feel welcome. But then...

He gasps, and I can tell from those breathy moans he's getting close.

and then... oh fuck, I can't stop thinking about it... and then there's his sister.

I sit up, wide awake now, staring at the door. What the fuck? Panic
takes over, but I keep listening. Surely he's not about to out me?

*She's in these plaid pajamas, her dark hair is bunched
up in this messy bun, she's rubbing her eyes like the cutest
little sleepyhead who just woke up from a nap and I...oh
fuck... and I get rock fucking hard.*

*When she sees her brother, she comes running over to
hug him. I know from what he told me they're super
close, and then he turns to introduce us and she takes one
look at me and she looks... she looks mad.*

*Not just mad. Like, furious. She just stares me down,
hands on hips, back nice and straight like 'who the fuck
are you' written all over her face.*

*And that's when I realise, oh shit, this isn't just my
friend's favourite family holiday, it's hers too, and here
I am ruining it by showing up unexpectedly. I'm not
family, she doesn't know me, I'm the fifth wheel.*

*Anyway, obviously his whole family ski, and being a
born and bred beach bum, I do not. Today, they're all*

out on the slopes and I'm just chilling here in the chalet.
And I realised it's the perfect place to record one of these
audios because it's all soft furnishings, gorgeous views.

So right now... fuck... oh shit, I'm really fucking hard.
I'm sitting on this big chaise longue, ...

My chaise longue? Did *Mac 'n 'Please* get himself off in my favourite
chair? I've stopped breathing. I'm going to die.

...and it's positioned right by these floor to ceiling win-
dows so I'm looking out across the slopes and it's so
fucking beautiful. Like something from a movie or a
fairytale. And everything covered in snow is so stunning.
So pure. Kind of makes me want to do really bad things.

And I keep thinking, what if she comes back? What if
she walks in here and finds me like this? My hand in
my sweatpants, my hard dick in my hand.

Would she like it?

Would she hate me even more?

Would she get on her knees and take me in her mouth?

I pause the audio, pull off my headphones, and stare at my phone. My heart races out of control, so loud I can hear it in my ears.

He's fucking with me, right?

Chapter 14

Hannah

Obviously, I listened to the rest of the audio. Then again when I woke up around five and couldn't fall back asleep.

Not only did I listen to him get himself off, but I listened as he described, in exquisite detail, all the things he'd like to do to his holiday housemate.

The housemate who happens to be me.

He didn't use my name, and for all his listeners know, the scenario was entirely fictional, but *I* know. I knew when he described the chaise, the view, his arrival.

I knew when he described my braids, and how much he wanted to wrap them around his fists as he pulled me down onto his cock.

And honestly? What the fuck am I supposed to do with that information?

Not keen to lie in bed overthinking things, I got up early and slipped out to visit the *boulangerie* for baguettes and croissants fresh from the oven. I needed space to think about what this all means.

Cameron, *Mac'n'Please*, knows who I am, knows I listen to his work, knows I'm attracted to him, and apparently he wants me, too. He's laying his cards on the table, in the way he communicates best, but something feels off. I know so much about him, and all he knows about me is I'm his best friend's sister, I'm a lawyer, and I know how to ski. None of that is enticing, which makes me wonder if he's just using the idea of me for content. That definitely doesn't do it for me.

Maybe his whole kink is hooking up with listeners. I've seen it happen with other creators, and it never ends well.

I may be shy, but I'm not a pushover. If he wants to taunt me, he won't get an easy fight.

My parents were awake when I got back, so I grabbed a coffee and helped Dad set out the breakfast things. Now I'm having my own private moment of contemplation, stretched out on the chaise.

Ordinarily the thought of anyone getting themselves off here would have me throwing up then reaching for a heavy duty upholstery cleaner, but knowing Cameron was here yesterday afternoon, alone and horny and thinking of me, is making me feral.

His move was a gamble. He has no way of knowing if I heard his audio, so I'm desperate for him to wake up so I can get a read on him.

My heart rate quickens when I hear a door open on the upstairs landing, but the feet that come down the stairs belong to my brother. He grunts in my direction as he heads for the kitchen.

Thankfully, I don't have to wait much longer, and he appears a few minutes later, still in pyjamas and a t-shirt, one hand scratching softly through his mussed up hair.

"Morning, Hannah."

"Good morning, Cameron."

"Did you sleep well?" he asks, a broad, knowing grin stretched across his face.

"Yes, thank you." I hope he barely slept a wink, the cheeky fucker. "I listened to some music, woke up super relaxed."

"Oh, that's nice," he cocks his head to one side, eyes on me. "What did you listen to?"

"I don't think you'd have heard of it." I take a slow sip of my coffee and refuse to look away.

"I have pretty varied tastes."

"It's kind of niche."

"Try me."

"Why are you being weird?" Ryan interrupts our stand-off, tearing off a hunk of baguette and smothering it with jam. "We all know it was probably Taylor Swift."

"Hey," Cameron snaps at him. "Watch your mouth, bro. Nothing wrong with a bit of Taylor."

Chapter 15

Cameron

"YOU FEEL YOU'VE GOT the hang of this now? Or do you want me to ask the liftie to slow it right down for us?"

"I think I'm pretty much an expert now." The way she rolls her eyes at my bragging is so damn cute. We shuffle forward in the line, bumping our wrists against the lift pass scanner as we approach the turnstile.

"What's your favourite Taylor Swift song?" I ask once we're in the air. I learned fast that if I don't ask Hannah a question on the chairlift, she'll stay quiet the entire time. It's not that I think she's a shy person, I think she just forces herself to keep her mouth shut around me.

What I really want to ask is if she listened to the audio I uploaded yesterday, but I only had to take one look at her sipping her coffee on the chaise this morning and I knew she had. So Taylor Swift it is.

"Don't be ridiculous," she laughs, wiggling her hips as she gets comfy in the chair. "One does not simply have a *favourite* Taylor Swift song. It changes day by day and mood by mood."

"Do you have a favourite audio of mine?" *Oops. There goes my resistance.*

"What did you say?"

"What else do you listen to?" I try not to smirk, but pretty sure she narrows her eyes at me from behind her goggles. I can practically hear her brain whirring as she thinks about how to respond. As much as it's fun to play with her, I don't want to push her even further away. Now seems as good a time as any to clear the air.

"Hannah," I tuck my ski poles under my thigh, the way she showed me, then lean a little closer so I can lift her goggles up and rest them on top of her helmet. Her eyes meet mine as she sucks in her breath and holds it there. "I know you know who I am."

Her mouth parts, closes softly, then parts again. I'm dying to hear her admit it, but she looks away, and pulls her goggles back down.

Fuck. I've lost her.

"I'm not trying to embarrass you," I say. "It would be hypocritical for me to judge the very people I make content for."

She turns away, arms folded across her chest.

"Come on, admit it."

"Fine," she says, sighing with her whole body. "I know who you are."

"Finally," I nudge up against her shoulder with mine. "So glad we got that off our chests."

"Was it the DMs?" she asks. "Is that how you figured it out?"

"It was the DMs."

She groans and buries her face in her hands. "I am mortified. I was trying to delete them."

"Why? I told you. You have nothing to be embarrassed about."

"I just..." She shakes her head and her silence gives way to nervous laughter.

"Just what?"

"I still can't believe this is happening. I thought your name was Mac. I assumed it was short for MacKenzie or MacDonald or something."

"Mac is Cam spelled backwards," I clarify.

"Oh. So it is. But you're not Mac. You're a real person, and you're here. In my chalet. I never thought you'd read those messages, far less turn up in my actual life. It's awkward as fuck."

"I don't think it's awkward."

She shifts to face me. "You don't think it's awkward that your friend's little sister listens to your audio porn and then messages you to tell you how hard she came? And now you're stuck on holiday with her, sleeping on the other side of her bedroom wall for two weeks?"

"I particularly enjoyed the ones about how hard you came." My dick twitches in my ski pants at the memory of her words.

> *'You're a menace. You made me come in under a minute and I had to pause the rest of the audio to recover.'*

"We're not talking about this," she says, shuffling to face forward again.

We'll see.

I'm not going to push her, and we're nearing the top of the lift, but this conversation is far from over. We hop off at the same time and ski clear of the exit path and crowds reading piste maps, coming to a stop by a treeline near the top of the slope.

"Does Ryan know about... what you do?" Hannah asks, fiddling with the velcro strap of her gloves.

"Yeah, he knows. He's cool with it."

Her eyes snap up to mine. "Oh my God, does he do this too? Please tell me I haven't come to my brother's voice."

That would be pretty fucking awkward. I know a few other voice actors well enough to chat online, but most keep their identity a closely guarded secret. Some have government jobs, or wives and kids who don't know about their side-hustle. It's bound to have happened, a listener getting off to someone they know in real life. A co-worker. A friend. Their kid's teacher.

"Nah, not as far as I'm aware. He's a busy boy, doesn't have the time. Or the creative talent."

She slides over to a nearby tree and screams. A bird flaps free from the branches and flies off.

"Feel better?"

"No," she says with an angry grunt. "So Ryan knows about you, and I know about you, but Ryan doesn't know I know about you. Right?"

"Correct."

"Can we please keep it that way?" she asks, desperately.

"Of course. We don't talk about that side of my work much."

"OK. I'm just mortified. And I'd be so ashamed if he knew."

She's spiralling, getting herself worked up over nothing. I use my ski poles to push myself round in front of her, positioning my skis on either side of hers. It feels bold, caging her in like this, but she doesn't back away. "There's nothing to be ashamed of. You're a beautiful woman who enjoys taking some time to prioritise her own pleasure. My work is literally created for that purpose. You've done nothing wrong."

She's so fucking beautiful. The way she blushes, the way her teeth catch her lip, the way she inhales slowly, gathering her thoughts, holding something back. Not for the first time, I wonder what she'd be like if she was completely uninhibited, completely herself. Could I get her to bite her lip that way while holding back a moan? Could I get her to beg for what she wants? I'd sure as hell give it my best shot.

"Nothing wrong with you," I whisper.

I want to kiss her.

I *could* kiss her, right here, but there's every chance she'd push me over the edge of the slope and I'd never be seen again. Or she wouldn't push me, but I'd embarrass her more, and she'd retreat even further. Neither option is good. I have plenty of time with her, and if something happens, something happens.

"I tell you what," I say, holding both ski poles in one hand so I can rest the other on her shoulder. "I have one more question, then we can stop talking about this, unless you want to bring it up again."

A long pause hangs in the air between us. I want the ball in her court, but her silence tells me she doesn't want to end this conversation at all.

"OK. What's the question?"

"Did you enjoy my latest audio?"

Hannah gasps, her mouth opening and closing, cheeks blooming as she struggles to articulate her response. I won't make her suffer any longer.

"Thought so," I say, unable to hide my smile. I want to touch her so fucking badly. I settle for a tug on one of her pigtails. "Race you to the bottom. Loser buys lunch."

"Fondue on you then," she laughs, shoving her fists against my chest to push clear of my skis. "Don't get yourself lost."

Then she's off. Braids whipping behind her, laughter on the breeze, strong legs carrying her away. And all I can do is follow and try to keep up.

Mac 'n' Please

At the Bar

I swear I don't normally do this and I'm not some serial killer stalker who invites women back to his apartment or anything.

OK, I guess that is what a killer would say. Sorry, I'm kind of nervous. I honestly don't do this.

Do you want to... I don't know... take a picture of me and send it to everyone you know along with my address so they know where you are? I'll give you my number, my social security, anything you need to feel safe here.

You do? Good. I should shut up then, right?

OK. How about you come over here and make me shut up.

Chapter 16
Hannah

"ARE YOU KIDS HEADING out tonight?" Dad asks as we finish up the tiramisu Mum picked up from the *patisserie* this afternoon.

"Rico's," I nod around my last spoonful.

"Well be safe and let me know if you're staying out after midnight." He stands to clear our empty plates.

"What do you have planned?" I ask.

"Hot tub under the stars with your beautiful mother," he says, bending to press a kiss to the top of her head. My default reaction is to cringe, but the way she smiles up at him is contagious. Most of my friends' parents have been through messy divorces, and I've seen plenty of shitstorms go down at work. I'm no expert at relationships, there's comfort in knowing my parents are still happily in love after so many years together.

I can only hope I find a love like theirs one day.

"I'll go grab the sledges," Ryan says, and Cameron looks between me and Ryan's retreating figure, his brow knitting together in that way I'm obsessed with.

"Rico's bar is in the next village. We get the late lift up then sledge home."

"You're messing with me."

"I'm not," I laugh. "There's a road, but waiting for a taxi is boring, so we slide home. We've done it for years."

—ele—

Rico's is already busy by the time we get there, and while Ryan heads for the bar, Cameron and I hunt for a table, weaving our way through to a small one with high stools near the back. I hang my coat over my seat and hop up.

Mountain bars are nothing like city bars. You can't exactly dress up in a skirt and heels here, unless you're willing to freeze to death on the way home. Most people are in ski pants and t-shirts or hoodies. We're no different, though Cameron opted for a soft plaid shirt open over his plain white t-shirt. The kind of shirt I'd love to wrap myself up in.

"So, do you come here often?" Cameron asks, then scrunches his nose, wincing at the dated pickup line that happens to be a genuine question.

"It's a pilgrimage, I suppose." I'm tucked into the wall side of a corner table, and while I have a view of the bar, Cameron's eyes are all on me and I feel far too warm because of it. "When we were kids, we'd stop off for pizza after a day on the slopes, but as we got older we were allowed to stay back with our friends. They weren't so hot on checking for ID back then, which helped."

"Were you a wild child?" he asks, wiggling his eyebrows. The idea is laughable. Goody-two shoes Hannah was so far from wild.

"Not at all. I was always the one making sure nobody got too drunk and everyone made it home safe."

"You know many people here?"

I glance around over his shoulder. "I recognise a few, but a lot of our friends stopped coming out once they got older. They get jobs, start families of their own, properties get sold. But it was a dream to spend Christmases here as a child. We've had some amazing times."

I zone out a little, memories rushing to the surface. Learning to ice-skate on the frozen lake, our evening walks to see all the local families' nativity displays, which seemed to get grander and grander each year. The Santa parade through town was always a highlight, with shop-owners dressing as elves to hand out sweets to the children they passed. Everyone went to great lengths making it a magical time, but Christmas, like life I guess, loses a little of its sparkle once you get older.

"What about you?" I ask.

"What about me?"

"Were you a wild child?"

"Not at all. Good as gold," Cameron grins.

I tip my head to one side. "I find that hard to believe."

"Why?"

"Well... just... you know."

"No, I don't know. Come on, why is it so hard to believe I'm a good boy?"

"I've heard you say plenty of things that suggest otherwise."

"Any highlights?"

"Um..." He's so casual in the way he asks, as if this is a perfectly normal thing for two people to be discussing over a beer in a bar. He's so relaxed about the whole thing that it makes me think I could tell him.

I could tell him I love his audio about co-workers trapped in the back room of a bookstore overnight. I could tell him that the way he takes control in Summer Nights altered my brain chemistry. That his Good Grades series lives in my brain rent free.

"What do you like, Hannah?" he asks again, leaning in. My body follows his instinctively, swaying forward, lured in by the seduction in his voice.

"I like..."

A packet of fried potato chips lands on the table between us, dropped straight from between my brother's teeth. His hands balance three beer glasses in a careful triangle. I snap out of my Cameron induced trance and lean back, tearing open the packet and spreading it out flat for us to share.

"Anyone for a game?" Ryan pulls a deck of cards from his pocket. "I think it's about time we beat Cam's ass at L'Escalier."

"What the hell is L'Escalier?" Cameron asks, sitting back as the tension between us fizzles away.

"We don't really know," I laugh. "Mum and Dad taught us, but we have yet to meet a single other person who's even heard of it."

"You'll love it though. It's easy to pick up," Ryan reassures him as he deals three hands of eight cards and places the rest in a pile between us.

An hour, two beers, and five rounds later, Cameron almost beats me but I play an ace at the last second and win.

"*No.* That was brutal! I was so close, I was sure I had it that time."

I hold my hands to the sky. "That's L'Escalier. Close isn't always close enough." Beneath the table, Cameron's knee nudges against mine.

"I need to pee," Ryan says, hopping down from his stool. "The next win is mine."

Cameron gathers our cards and shuffles, his long fingers making swift work of the deck. I watch them as he deals three new piles, thumb sliding card after card from the top. It's impossible not to imagine him touching me that way, a firm but smooth, repetitive motion building me up until I see stars. Imagine that thumb on my lip, or pressing into the flesh of my thigh.

It's uncontrollable, this urge to fantasise about him. I mean, I was already doing that before I even flew out here, now that he's around all the time it's impossible to stop. I keep my mouth shut, in case the beer loosens my lips a little too much and I say something I can't take back. He finishes dealing, sits back and sips his beer, but when our eyes lock I get the feeling he's holding back from saying something too.

Ryan appears at the side of the table with his arm around the shoulders of a familiar petite brunette. "Change of plans."

"Hi, Kayla," I smile and wave from my seat in the corner.

"Hey, Hannah," she replies, a knowing smile. "It's good to see you."

"You too. You here for the holidays?"

"I live here full time now, actually. Started my touring business. Snow in the winter, bikes in the summer."

"That's fantastic news. Congratulations." I mean it. It's wonderful to see her follow her dreams. She's always fit right in here, and as kids she was always heartbroken to go home to the UK and back to school.

"Kayla, this is my buddy Cameron," Ryan says. Cameron twists to offer his hand and Kayla reaches out to shake it, leaving her other wrapped around my brother's waist. "We flew out together, and he's staying for Christmas and New Year with us. Cameron, this is Kayla."

"Good to meet you. You joining us for a game?"

She tilts her head to look at Ryan, eyes sparkling. "Er..."

"We're gonna head off actually," he smiles down at her. "I'll see you losers in the morning."

And then they're gone, leaving the two of us alone. Part of me is grateful I don't have to watch what I say in front of my brother anymore. The other part is terrified that without his buffer, I might start saying things I regret and never stop talking.

"You know her?" Cameron asks.

"Her family owns a few properties, so she's here most winters. She teaches snowboarding."

"And she and your brother are...?"

"Getting reacquainted, apparently." I smile and raise my glass to my lip. "They do this a lot. She was pretty gutted he didn't make it out last winter."

Ryan's made no secret of his feelings for Kayla, and the same goes for her. When they reunite on the mountain, it's like watching a fireworks display. Explosive, magnificent, and then over with only a trail of smoke left behind. He once told me they check in during the off-season, but I have to wonder what's going to happen the year he turns up and finds her committed to someone else.

Cameron nudges my knee again. "So it looks like it's just you and me, kid."

"Don't call me kid," I scowl.

"What would you prefer I call you?" He leans in closer, the bass of the music, the chatter of the crowd all blending into one as he whispers inches from my face. "Baby? Darling? Good girl? Greedy little slut?"

It could be my shaky gasp that gives it away, or my teeth sinking into my lip, or the way my eyes roll back. Probably all three.

"The last one," he nods to himself, leaning back on his barstool, eyes locked on mine as he drains his glass. "Noted. You want another?"

I still have half a beer left. "I'm not sure that's such a good idea."

"Another drink, or staying out with me?"

"Maybe both," I laugh nervously. "I'm not a big drinker."

"OK, so let's get you home."

"You don't need to cut your night short for me."

"You'd leave your guest unaccompanied, halfway up a mountain, in a country he doesn't know?"

"You're a big boy. I'm sure you can handle it," I say. He raises his eyebrows, smirking at my unintentional innuendo, and heat creeps further up my neck.

"More to the point, *I* wouldn't let a beautiful woman make her way home from a bar alone on a cold, dark mountain. If you get eaten by a bear, I'd never be able to live with myself."

"There are no bears here," I laugh.

"Maybe someone else will eat you."

Heat spreads through my belly, pooling low and deep in my core. I don't know whether it's my dirty mind, scrambled by hours spent listening to him talk about how much he likes to go down on a woman, or if he's really being this direct with me.

He helps me into my coat, his firm hands squeezing my shoulders and stroking down my arms. I feel his touch everywhere. A spark between us threatening to catch.

"So how do we do this?" he says, holding his sledge in his hands at the top of the slope. They're not much more than a plastic disk with a handle, but they get the job done.

"You've never been sledging?"

"On those famous snowy Los Angeles mountains?" he teases. "No, I haven't. I mean, we do actually have mountains in L.A. now that I think about it, but I've never been. Plenty of hikes, but we weren't exactly a family of adventurers. I'm not sure my mom has ever even left the state of California. She'd probably have an aneurysm if she saw me right now. Maybe I should call her, say goodbye, you know?"

"Cameron," I put my hand on his arm and he stops. "You're rambling. Are you OK?"

"Why am I so nervous?" he laughs. "Oh yeah, because I'm about to throw myself down a dark mountain on a piece of plastic that barely takes one ass cheek, that's why."

"I'll keep you safe. Here, let me show you how it's done." I sit down, wiggling a little to get myself centred with the loop handle pulled up between my legs. Beside me, Cameron does the same. "OK now we just scoot up to the edge of the slope but dig your heels in so you don't go yet."

"There are no brakes on this thing?"

"It's easy. Once you get going, lift your feet up. If you want to slow down, put them flat and pull the handle up towards yourself. If you need to adjust course, lean your body in the opposite direction to where you want to go."

"Maybe we should just call a taxi?"

"Cameron, you can do this. It's the quickest way, and it's not far. I promise you'll be fine. Just follow me."

Chapter 17

Cameron

"SLOW DOWN!" HANNAH SCREAMS behind me, but it's too late. The second I lifted my feet, I zoomed straight past her. I've veered off to the edge of the slope, and no matter which way I lean, I can't get myself right again. Trees zip past in my peripheral vision, and I'm certain no other human has ever gone this fast before.

"Use your feet," I hear her shout, but that only serves to catapult me over the bank of snow at the edge of the slope and then I'm flying. I land face first, inches from the base of a tree.

I hear her boots a few seconds later, stomping up the bank until she comes into view, dropping to her knees at my side. "Are you OK?"

"I did not expect it to go that fast." I laugh, then cough and wheeze a little. That'll hurt tomorrow.

"Are you hurt?"

"I don't think so."

I roll to my back, and she brushes the snow from my front. Her mittens sweep across my jacket and then down over my crotch and my thighs. My hips have a mind of their own, tipping upwards, but she's too busy rescuing me to realise she's basically rubbing my dick. She brings her hands up to my face and neck, her fingers digging out where snow has packed inside my collar. It's ice cold, but all I feel is warmth looking up at her like this.

I wrap my hand around her wrist and hold it there by my throat, wishing we weren't wearing gloves. Too many layers between us. She stills, her breath a soft cloud in the cold air. Even in the darkness, hidden underneath the low branches, I can make out the fullness of her lips, the pink of her cold nose.

"You still didn't answer my question."

"What question?"

"About your favourite audio of mine."

Her breath shudders, only making me more desperate to know. "You want to talk about this *now*?"

"I want to talk about it until I get an answer."

"Fine," she huffs, scooting back to lean against the trunk of the tree. "I like your confessions."

"The *Can I Tell You Something?* series?"

"Yes."

"What do you like about them?" She stares at me, that cute fucking glare, but I can tell she's dying to say more. I crawl into the space next to her and take a seat, too. "Come on, it's not often I get to ask a fan straight up for feedback."

"You dick," she says, throwing a clump of snow at my chest. "I'm not a fan."

"Your DMs suggest otherwise."

"Argh," she covers her face with her hands. I shouldn't be pushing this. Getting involved with listeners has never worked out well, but there's something different about Hannah.

I could have written off my initial attraction to her as thinking with my dick, but when I read those DMs something shifted.

Yes, she was flirty with her feedback, but she was also appreciative and complimentary. Her messages made me feel like she sees me as a person, not just a hot voice to get off to.

I'm throwing myself down a goddamn mountain for this woman, but the way she's looked after me the past couple of days, I couldn't feel safer. She's got me breaking my rules, and I can't seem to stop myself.

"Come here." I pull her sideways into my lap, and to my relief, she doesn't resist. "I told you, nothing to be embarrassed about. You can tell me."

"I guess... I like that they're real. You're not playing a part, and there's a vulnerability there."

"What else?"

"I enjoy hearing about things you've done. Things you want to do."

"What else?"

"I like hearing you moan."

"Mmmm." It's not deliberate, I can't help it. She's making me moan, and she's not even touching me. "Can I tell you something I want to do?"

"Uh-huh." She sinks a little lower into me, her forehead dropping to mine. I let the moment linger, fully aware there's no turning back.

"I really want to kiss you, Hannah. Been wanting to do it since I first laid eyes on you."

"OK," she whispers on an exhale.

"OK?"

"Ye—" I cut her off with a tilt of the head, my lips pressed to hers at last. Soft at first, until I feel her kissing me back. I have no restraint when she opens for me, her warm tongue slipping past my lips to meet mine. She's warm and soft and tastes like heaven. I embarrass myself, getting instantly hard beneath her thigh but when I try to reposition her she shifts more, lifting one leg until she's sinking down to straddle me and - *oh my fuck that feels good.*

One hand grips my jacket as she pulls me closer into her, the other cupping the back of my neck, claiming me. I thought she'd be soft and demure, but the way she sucks my bottom lip into her mouth and sinks her teeth into it makes me think I was sorely mistaken about Hannah.

Jesus, I could never write a kiss as good as this.

My hands find her hips, but these fucking gloves are in the way. I pull them off and push my hands up underneath her ski jacket, pulling at her clothes until they meet bare skin. She cries into my mouth as my hands push higher, fingertips meeting the soft swell of her tits under thin lace. I take a firm handful, thumb grazing over her tight nipple and she rolls her hips, throws her head back and —

Above us, there's a creak, then a crack, a rush of sound and a muffled whomp as the tree we're huddled under drops a curtain of snow.

Instinctively, I pull Hannah tight into my body, wrapping my arm around her head to tuck it to my chest. I keep her there until I dare open my eyes and assess our situation. It was already dark, but I can see even less now, a mound of powder built up all around us. As much as I don't want to, I lift Hannah off of me and crawl as far as I can, scooping snow out of the way until there's a gap we can fit through.

"This mountain is trying to kill me," I say, looking back at where she's waiting, fingers pressed to her lips, flushed pink from my kisses. "Let's get you home before we get trapped here and freeze to death."

Chapter 18
Hannah

"WHAT'S THE PLAN FOR today, then?" Dad asks from across the breakfast table where we've mostly eaten in silence.

Personally, my plan is to try to keep my shit together and not mount Cameron every chance I get.

What happened last night has been replaying on a constant loop in my head. The way his lips felt pressed against mine, the mix of beer and salt on his tongue as it coaxed into my mouth. The way his fingers curled around my pigtail, tugging my head back, then holding me tight to his chest as snow fell around us. The way my ear pressed against his chest in just the right spot to hear his heartbeat race.

It was a Hollywood level kiss.

And that was just the first one. We walked the rest of the way home in silence, arm in arm, but the second we stepped back into the chalet, his mouth was on mine again. My back against the wall, his hands unzipping my coat, pushing it from my shoulders and finding a new home on my waist, as mine raked through those curls I've longed to take hold of.

His tongue found my lips, teasing them apart on an urgent mission to stroke into my mouth. Our hands were everywhere, frantic and desperately seeking more skin. My fingertips curled around the muscles of his back, while his slid up and up, underneath my t-shirt until they found the curve of my breasts, a trail of goosebumps flushing over my skin.

His hips ground against me with an upward thrust and a deep moan, followed by a garbled one from me as my brain processed the sensation of him hard against my zipper.

When we pulled apart, both panting for breath, he held my face in his hands and stared into my eyes, pupils blown and needy.

"We need to get you into bed."

"Yours?" I sighed, pressing my hips back against his.

"No way. What if your brother comes home? Or we might wake your parents."

I hadn't imagined he would be so cautious. It caught me off guard as I reconfigured the pieces of my brain that imagined him as an exhibitionist thrill-seeker willing to fuck anywhere and everywhere with the true pieces of the man stood in front of me.

"Not tonight. But soon," he'd moaned into my mouth. He squeezed my ass as I climbed the stairs first, then apologised softly in the darkness. I'd have let him touch me anywhere. At my door he pressed a kiss to my forehead, whispered *'see you in the morning'*, then slipped past me and closed the door to his room gently. And there he stayed, despite my hopes he'd sneak out at some point, into my room, where he'd find me underneath the covers, needy and waiting for his touch.

It was a clear boundary. Not around my brother, and not around my parents, which suits me fine, but in the cold light of day I'm freaking out about how I'm supposed to handle this.

Cameron is all man, pure sexual magnetism. Those gorgeous curls, that beautiful smile that literally makes me feel like my underwear is disintegrating. Even if I didn't know about him from his *Mac 'n' Please* audios, it's impossible not to look at him and feel turned on.

I wasn't lying when I said *Can I Tell You Something?* is my favourite series. I've listened to countless hours of him telling me, well, his listeners, what he's into. How he likes to touch himself, his favourite positions, all the little things that turn him on. Nobody knows better than me how skilled and adventurous he is in the bedroom.

I know he likes to be dominant most of the time, but switch it up occasionally and let his partners take control, too. He finds confident women a turn on, especially when they tell him what they want. I know he gets off on his partner's pleasure, enjoys a little BDSM, and has no problem having sex in public.

Compared to all that, I'm just... me.

I've only slept with a handful of men, and one was, in hindsight, so selfish in the bedroom I'm not sure he touched my clit once in the time we were together. I've never asked for anything in my life, and I've only ever had sex in a bed. That's probably Cameron's fifth favourite place to do it.

I might have a sense in my mind of what I enjoy, but I'm nowhere near as confident or experienced as him. Last night was hot as hell, but what will he think of me when he finds out I don't know what I'm doing? What would he even want with someone like me?

The unfortunate reality is he probably hooks up with women everywhere he goes, and I just happen to be the woman who is here right now. An easy target. A one-night thing for him is my every fantasy coming to life. And then what? I'd never recover. I'd certainly not be able to come back to this house again knowing what we'd done in it.

He knows from my messages how I feel about him, but he doesn't know I'm basically obsessed. Thankfully, I had the sense not to declare my undying love over what I thought was a one-sided Instagram DM chat. Then I really would throw myself off the edge of a crevasse.

But then I remember the words he whispered last night as he lifted my chin... '*I really want to kiss you*' and '*been wanting to do it since I first laid eyes on you*'. Was that true, or is it something he says to every woman he meets?

Plus, there's the small matter of him being friends with my brother, and the fact he lives on the other side of the world. Am I supposed to kiss him goodbye and pretend nothing ever happened between us? That kiss was unlike any I've had in my life, and it's hard to believe it could be better with anyone else.

Oh God, this is a living nightmare. I'm on a one-way train to Heartbreak town.

"Hellooo?" Dad says again. "Today? Plans? Does anyone have any?"

"French onion soup." Ryan and I say at exactly the same time.

"A most excellent plan," Mum says. "I think Dad and I will join you."

"Is this magic soup or something?" Cameron laughs, loading his plates into the dishwasher.

"The French onion soup at The Marmot is an event, Cameron," Mum explains. "We take a telecabin lift to the top of the mountain and ski back down after lunch."

"Do you think I'll be able to handle it, teach?" Cameron says, dropping his hand on my shoulder as he stands behind me. My eyes shoot up towards Ryan, who's thankfully too busy looking at his phone to notice, then to Mum, who has her back turned as she clears the table. Cameron sweeps his thumb up the side of my neck and a shiver rolls through me.

I am so fucked.

Then he's gone, lifting his hand to walk around to the other side of the table. I keep my head down but coast my eyes up at him. God, he's cute, his hair all mussed up, his stubble a little more rugged than usual. I wonder if he got any sleep, or if thoughts similar to mine kept him awake.

"It's a red run home, but I think you'll manage if you take it slow."

"What if I want to go fast?" he says with a wink so sexy it should be illegal. "What do they say, go hard or go home? I want to go hard today."

'What are you doing?' I mouth, my thighs pressing together underneath the table.

'What?' he mouths back and shrugs, like he's not flirting with me right in front of my entire family. He fishes his phone from his pocket and, a few seconds later, mine lights up on the table beside me.

I grab it and swipe open the notification.

Cam: I can't stop thinking about last night. Can we find some time alone today?

Oh shit. I don't know how to play this.

"We could get a few runs in this morning and meet everyone there for lunch?"

"Sounds great." He steps behind Ryan and gives his shoulders a squeeze. "You joining us, man?"

"Nah, bro, gonna meet up with Kayla before her classes this morning."

"Oh, what a shame," Cameron says, staring right at me with a wolfish grin on his face. "Hannah, are you coming?"

This is torture.

Chapter 19

Hannah

"THIS IS A BAD idea. *You* are a bad idea," I whisper loudly, stomping away from the house as quickly as my ski boots allow.

"What did I do?"

"Flirting in front of my brother, sneaking around, looking at me like you're thinking about me naked. You're not very subtle."

"I *am* thinking about you naked, but nobody knows except you. Your brother has barely stopped looking at his phone since he got home. And anyway..." he says, throwing his arm around my shoulder. "Isn't there something kind of hot about sneaking around?"

The penny drops. Of course, that's all he sees me as, someone to sneak around with. A quick and dirty fling. I shrug him off and march on towards the lift at the base station at the end of our road. "Someone might see us."

"So what?"

So what? Is he serious?

I don't sneak around with men, and certainly not while my parents are in the same house. I know I'm freaking out, but I'm still getting used to the fact that Cameron is even here in my presence, let alone hitting on me and touching me whenever he wants. It feels like I'm a pathetic little fan girl and I'm sure I won't be the first listener he's been intimate with.

The crowds are bigger today and we push our way onto the packed telecabin, jostling with armpits, backpacks, skis and snowboards to find some space. Cameron loops his arm around my shoulders and pulls me into his body. I let him hold me there as the doors close and we sweep out of the station and up the mountain.

I stare out of the window at the view as we climb higher. It's not like I know everyone in town, but I know some people, and I have no idea how I would explain this if they recognised him.

Oh God, what if someone recognises Cameron here when I'm with him?

If I found him online, it stands to reason that others will have too. He has thousands of followers on his Instagram. Not celebrity levels, but I'm sure he gets spotted plenty.

When we exit onto the slope, I lead him across the plateau, weaving through the crowds towards the next chairlift. It's a two-seater that will carry us up to a peak where we can take one of several blue runs down into a valley and get some practice in before lunch.

Dropping my skis to the ground, I click my boots into place and Cameron follows as we shuffle into place, letting the chairlift scoop us up. He's got the technique nailed now, tucking his poles underneath his thigh as he reaches up to help me pull the safety bar down.

"Are you ashamed to be seen with me?" he says, his shoulders slumping forward. He sounds sad, and that's not what I intended at all.

"No, it's just..." I twist my body towards him and wish I could see him properly underneath his goggles. "This is so awkward."

"Because we kissed?"

"Yes," I admit, even though not one part of me ever wanted those kisses to end. "And because you came here with my brother."

"So you *are* ashamed of me?"

"No, but what are the chances? I don't think he'd be thrilled about this."

"Hmmm, he told me to stay away from you, actually."

"He said that?" I say, snapping my head towards him.

"I assumed he was just playing the protective big brother role. I didn't think I'd get here and his sister would be *you*. I never thought you'd know who I am."

"How on earth are we supposed to explain this? I don't want my brother to know I know about Mac. I mean, we're close, but we're not *swapping masturbation material* close."

"We could tell him it's an undeniable physical attraction. Which, on my part, is 1000% true."

Sure, me and who else, my brain helpfully chimes in.

"I'm not some desperate fangirl, and I apologise if I've given you that impression. I don't want to be another notch on your bedpost."

"Hannah, look at me," he says, straightening up. "I don't do this. I don't hook up with fans, but I was attracted to you before I knew you were aware of my work."

"What do you mean, you don't hook up with fans?"

He shrugs. "I don't know how else to say it. I don't sleep with listeners."

"But you said... what about *The Convention*?" He goes to a conference for voice actors and ends up taking a fan back to his hotel room and whispering all her favourite lines in her ear while he fucks her over the back of a sofa. It's one of my favourites.

Who am I kidding? The man doesn't miss. They're all my favourites. "You talked about sleeping with a fan in that audio."

"Those audios aren't real. They're stories. I make them up. That's a fantasy lots of my listeners have, and I like to make content that fulfils those desires, but that's all it is, a fantasy. Most of those scenarios I've talked about have only ever happened in my head. And I definitely don't go to conventions."

"Oh." The weight of the conversation shifts, then lifts slightly as his words sink in. I've taken everything in his content at face value, fully swept into his filthy world. It's never occurred to me it wasn't all based on reality, but what he's saying now is the truth. He doesn't sleep with listeners, and this thing between us is crumbling fast.

"You really don't sleep with fans?"

"I won't lie to you. I have in the past, a couple of times, but it wasn't good. They think they know me based on what they've heard, or they want me to do things a certain way. It's a weird dynamic. Honestly, I felt pretty used, so I made a rule not to get involved with listeners again. A rule you've got me dying to break."

"I'm sorry, that's awful. And I'm sorry for the times I've behaved inappropriately too. Some of those messages I sent you were really not OK. I was not in my right mind."

"You're off the hook," he says, but my actions dwell in my mind. I'd never be so bold to approach him in public, but I've said some pretty outrageous things to his veil of online anonymity online. Am I really any better than those women? And if he's telling me the truth, then who is the man behind the voice, the one sitting next to me right now? I barely know him at all.

"Don't go quiet on me," he says, pulling my attention back to him. "What are you thinking?"

"I'm just getting this all straight in my head. Separating fact from fiction. There's a lot I thought was real. I fully believed you're out having incredible sex all the time."

"I have a great imagination, and I'm a good storyteller, but I'm not even that active. I'm not dating anyone."

"I should hope not after the way you kissed me last night," I say, playfully slapping his arm.

"I mean it," he says, grabbing my hand and holding it there. "I haven't even slept with anyone in over six months."

"Oh. Well, that's... not that long."

"How long has it been for you?" he asks.

"Um, a year. Maybe more."

He huffs out a heavy sigh. "That makes me so fucking mad. And also happy."

"What?"

"Happy that nobody else is touching you. Mad because your body is gorgeous. It deserves to be touched and worshipped and adored."

"You haven't even seen my body," I laugh nervously.

Cameron slips his gloved hand between my thighs and tugs me closer. "I've felt it, and I can't wait to feel more. And if you haven't been touched in that long, I bet you'll be so needy for me."

Oh, good God.

I know full well how good he is at getting me worked up into a desperate state. He's already started and if he keeps this up, there'll be no way I can stop this.

"How's that going to work if you don't get involved with your fans?"

"Thought you weren't a fan," he teases.

"Thought you said my DMs proved otherwise."

"Touché."

My mouth tightens into a pout as I try not to smile.

"The thing is, you're not like other girls, Hannah," he says, then cringes. "Sorry, that's such a gross line. What I mean is, you knew who I was when I arrived here, but you didn't say a thing. If I hadn't figured it out, I'm pretty sure you'd have kept that to yourself this entire trip, right?"

"God, yes, I never wanted you to find out."

"That's how you're different. You showed me respect, you gave me space, let me be myself. Other women might have thrown themselves at me, seen me as a challenge and tried to seduce me." A small growl rumbles from my chest. "What was that? Do I detect a hint of jealousy?"

I don't like feeling this way, but I am. His content always centres the listener as the other partner in the story. I've imagined myself with him so often, but sharing is not something I'm interested in. "Of course I'm jealous."

"Hey can I ask you something? And feel free to tell me to get fucked if you don't want to talk about it."

I feel my shoulders physically tighten, lifting towards my ears as nervous anxiety kicks in. "Um, you can try me."

"Your brother mentioned an ex, a bad breakup. First, what a dick, but second, are you OK?"

I shift uncomfortably in the padded seat, but the safety bar keeps me pinned in place. "He told you about him?"

"Only very briefly, as part of the *'don't hit on my sister'* conversation. Do you want to talk about it at all? You don't have to."

"Two shitty exes, actually. They both cheated. It was a long time ago, and yes, the aftermath was a bad time for me. We don't even speak their names in our family. I have a lot of trust issues because of it, but I am OK. It's all in the past."

"I'm glad to hear that," he says.

"I think that's why Ryan pulls the big brother act sometimes. He, my most recent ex, was a friend of Ryan's, and I think he blames himself for what happened."

"Did this guy hurt you?"

"Not physically, no. And honestly, I am fine. I've been with a few other guys since—"

"OK," Cameron interrupts, laughing. "That's enough about the dumb idiots you've dated. I'm here to rescue you now."

"Oh thank goodness," I fawn, mocking him. "My knight in shining ski gear?"

"You're so fucking cute, you know that? Come here." He reaches for my cheek and leans in for a kiss, but our helmets bump together and when he tilts for a better angle, we butt heads again.

"Stupid helmets," he laughs and I can't help the smile that spreads across my face. "I'm banking that kiss for later."

"Promise?"

"Hannah, I want you naked the first chance I get. If we weren't on a chairlift right now, you wouldn't have a scrap of clothing on you."

"Oh."

"And hey, the scenarios are made up, but the moves are all mine. I promise I'll take good care of you."

Ohhh.

Chapter 20
Hannah

I'm adding The Marmot to my list of Happy Places.

Specifically, the deckchairs on the balcony at The Marmot, with a belly full of hearty French onion soup topped with gooey Gruyère toast, and the low buzz you get from precisely one glass of champagne.

It's a perfect bluebird day, with not a cloud in the sky. I bask in the warm sun as the beats of Lo-Fi house music float down from the bar slightly up the hill. Cameron has thankfully kept his hands to himself over lunch, bar the occasional knock of his knee against mine when nobody is looking.

Even if he's not touching me, I'm tuned into his presence. Those soft waves springing back after a morning underneath his helmet, the furrow of his brow when he looks my way from behind his sunglasses. The fullness of his lower lip, the back of his neck, tan from our days beneath mountain sunshine. He kept up with me all morning as we worked our way down a few of the easier red runs, but, always cautious my brother could appear out of nowhere, I couldn't bring myself to do more than sneak a few quick kisses.

The tension between us is thrumming, so electric I could pick him out in a room while blindfolded.

When everyone has finished their drinks and taken a bathroom break, we carry our skis to the top of the Lièvre run and get ourselves clipped back into all our gear. I feel high and giddy. On thin mountain air, fizz, my family being all together, Cameron, and life in general.

We usually race to the bottom, but today I'm in no rush, wishing I could bottle this feeling and keep it with me as long as possible.

"Last one to the bottom is a rotten egg!" Mum shouts, zooming off before Dad even has his ski poles in each hand.

It used to drive me bananas when she said that. What kid wants to be a rotten egg? Now though, I like that she still says these silly things from our childhood, and in hindsight I can see it made us better, bolder, faster skiers.

"Oh, so *I'm* the rotten egg? Very nice, Cheryl!" Cameron shouts after her. Ryan and Dad follow her, leaving Cam and me alone at the top of the run. He bumps his shoulder with mine and I feel like perhaps I could lean in and kiss him. "Want to make a new rule?"

"Depends on the rule."

"Last one to the bottom gets a kiss?"

"Deal." I stamp my ski poles into the snow, fold my arms across my chest, refusing to budge an inch.

"You're not even gonna make me work for it?" he laughs.

"Nope."

Cameron ducks his head to angle it below my helmet, and then his mouth is on mine. Soft, warm, a moan slipping between his lips and into mine. "I want you so much."

"They'll be wondering where we are." I hate myself for saying it, but it's all I can think of.

"I'll take the blame. Pretend I fell. Then you can nurse me back to full fitness." He kisses me again, one arm looping behind my shoulders to pull me closer as I melt beneath his tongue. I was obsessed before I even met him. Now that I know he kisses like this, it's terrifying. I could lose myself in him.

"Get a room!" some kid yells as they sail past us, and we break apart. Cameron shakes his head in disbelief.

"That little cockblocker."

"Come on," I say, looping my poles back around my wrists. "I want to show you something."

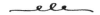

"Follow me," I call back up to him, pumping my right arm toward the woods that run along the side of the piste. I slow to a side slip as I approach, looking for a gap in the trees and when I find it, I zip between them.

"Oh, what the fuck," I hear him yell behind me a few seconds later.

"Just let your skis follow the tracks. And keep your head low."

Snaking through the woods is a hidden ski path, worn smooth by those who know it's here and protected from the sun's rays by the enormous pines above us. I weave in and out of trunks, ducking to avoid lower branches.

At a fork in the track, I veer right, leading us deeper into the woods until we reach a small clearing around an old stump. I think lightning hit it at one point, and now it's a hidden sanctuary, thick with several feet of snowpack under untouched powder.

"Holy shit, that was amazing!" He rests his hands on his knees, panting to get his breath back as adrenaline races through him. "My thighs are burning."

"I thought you'd like that. We always thought it was our special place when we were kids."

"Come here," he says, throwing his poles to one side and unbuckling his helmet. I do the same, hooking it over my wrist as he skis towards me, one of his sliding in between mine, the other to my side.

Our mouths crash together with equal force, both hungry after so many hours unable to get our fill of each other. His hands cup my face, tilting me up towards him while mine claw at the sides of his jacket, tugging him closer.

His kisses veer between soft and teasing, nipping at my lip, and desperate and searching, his tongue sweeping over mine.

He nudges me backwards, and I slide easily until my back hits the snowpack behind me. One hand cups the back of my head as he pins me in place with his knee and—

"Oh God, yes," I groan loudly.

"The knee thing?"

"The knee thing." I nod against his mouth, whimpering a little as he presses harder, dropping his kisses to my throat to suck gently at the tender skin there. My hips grind instinctively, desperate for friction, but between underwear, base layers and ski pants there are far too many layers between us. I want him to touch me so much I'm losing my mind.

"I need to get you alone," he huffs out, echoing my thoughts.

"We're alone right now," I whisper, dropping one hand to the hard bulge behind his zipper.

"Naked alone. And I don't know if that's wise out here in the cold." He's probably right. Here in the shade of the trees, the temperature feels much closer to freezing, not that you could tell from the way my blood pulses hot through my veins. "I want to do all kinds of things with you, but not here. Can we make that happen somehow?"

"I don't know," I sigh, dropping my forehead to his chest. "Someone is always around at the chalet."

He strokes my hair and sighs, too. "Fuck. I'm starving for you."

"Maybe we come back early one day? Or skip skiing altogether?"

He kisses me again, softer this time, and I close my eyes and let myself get lost in him. Cameron's kisses are a full body experience. Even when his mouth focuses on mine, his hands take care of the rest of me. They explore, play with my hair, grip my hip, squeeze my breast through my jacket, all a filthy taster of what he could really do to me if he had the chance.

"We'll find a way. I promise."

Chapter 21
Hannah

LUNCH AT THE MARMOT marks the start of the Richmond family Christmas traditions, and nobody is much inclined to keep skiing when we could be chilling out, eating, drinking, playing games, or taking afternoon naps as the night draws in.

Dad and I, however, have much more important plans.

"Hannah and I are off to do the big shop," he calls out to the entire house. "Anyone joining us?"

"No, boring," Ryan yells back from his bedroom. He's always preferred his food be delivered as directly to his mouth as possible. Doesn't care where it comes from or how it was made.

I, on the other hand, have year round dreams about French supermarkets. I picture myself roaming the aisles, filling my trolley with cheese, bread, and cured meats. I live for jars of rose petal jam, pistachio cream, and whipped hazelnut spread. And the crisps. Don't even get me started on the crisps. French crisp flavours are elite.

"I'll be spending the afternoon in the hot tub with a Nora Roberts secret baby romance if anyone needs me," Mum says, appearing in her bathrobe. Her Nora Roberts obsession was my gateway into romance novels, though the secret baby trope doesn't do it for me, personally.

"You want to come and see what the fuss is all about?" Dad asks Cameron, who is sitting at the dining table with his laptop.

"I have a bit of work to finish before tomorrow," he replies. "I'll see you when you get back."

"Suit yourself," Dad says.

Once Dad's back is turned, Cam blows a kiss in my direction, and I catch it in the air and smack it to my mouth like the sappiest, most love-drunk girl on the planet.

Truthfully, I'm glad he's staying behind. The pre-Christmas Big Shop has always been a Dad and me thing, even when I was a little girl. It's a twenty-minute drive down the mountain to the nearest town with a large supermarket and over the years we've accumulated a few traditions of our own. We sing along to the local radio station on the winding drive, a mix of songs in French and Christmas classics you'd hear in the UK too.

When my grandma was still with us we used her ancient deathtrap of a car, but we scrapped it after she died, and not a moment too soon. Dad now hires one at the airport, some heavy duty Land Rover type thing with snow tyres, heated seats, and that new car smell. And most importantly, plenty of space for all our shopping.

I ignore my phone on the drive in favour of the view, acutely aware of the fact that as my workload picks up, I might be in the same position as Ryan, unable to make it back for these trips every year. Up until now, they've always been a given, a privilege afforded to people with time off work, and parents who'll pay for the airfare. If I want to progress, I'll be expected to work all the hours of the day to prove my worth.

"What you thinking about, kiddo?" Dad asks as trees whizz past.

"Just work. How much I'll need to do to move up."

"You know my firm has your name on the door, right?" he teases.

"That's enough Dad, you know I want to get promoted on credibility, not nepotism. I've barely graduated and you're talking about partner. No pressure."

"You know that's been a dream of mine since you took an interest in law, but you've got plenty of time. Don't worry your life away on things you have no control over."

"I'm not doing that, Dad." I try my best to reassure him. "Honestly, I've been loads better."

"I know you have, darling, but I also know you've been working really hard. You're allowed to live a little."

I'm not lying. I am doing well, but even when I was at my lowest point, I constantly tried to convince my parents I was OK. When I couldn't get out of bed, when the thought of going to classes broke me out in a cold sweat. When it seemed like my only option was dropping out of university, or transferring to another school. When I cried all day, every day, I still said I was fine.

My breakdown happened when my second boyfriend, one of Ryan's old friends from school, broke my heart. When we ended up on the same course at university, we were an instant match. He was funny, handsome, smart, and loved by everyone we knew. I was besotted and set for life, or so I thought.

We dated through the first year, but when summer rolled around, he spent it not with me, but with another girl in our class. In Rome, the very city I'd suggested we visit together. I'd found out when she tagged him on her Instagram.

When I confronted him about it, he simply said he'd met someone else, and I should get over it. As if I could pretend my boyfriend hadn't cheated on me with my friend and not had the audacity to end it properly, almost exactly a year after my previous boyfriend had done something similar.

To have one man cheat on you is awful, but when it happens twice, well, then your brain is liable to convince you that you're not worth much.

I moped around the house all summer, then had my first panic attack the day school started again. I was terrified I'd see him, terrified I'd see her, convinced everyone was talking about me behind my back.

But that was a long time ago. I climbed out of that hole, spent some time with a therapist, and I vowed I'd never let a man come before my plans or my happiness again.

"As for this place, the house," Dad continues, "you can come here whenever you like. You and your brother. It will be yours when we're gone, and hopefully your kids after that one day."

"Kids? Partner? You need to slow down. Let me live a little," I tease, parroting his words.

While Dad finds a parking spot, I dig my phone out of the passenger side compartment and smile when I see a message from Cam.

Cam: Have a great afternoon x

Once we've parked, we grab the biggest trolley they have and make our way inside. The store is heaving with shoppers, but we don't mind. The longer the shop takes, the more random treats we get.

Dad has the shopping list for Christmas provisions, but I have a separate list in my head, purely for my own gastronomic pleasure.

We browse in silence, pointing out things we like the look of, marvelling at the quality of the fresh produce. Ripe tomatoes in deep reds and bright golds, artichokes the size of my face, endive lettuce and radishes in the richest pinks and purples.

Dad loads up on potatoes, herbs, and green beans before we head to the poultry counter to find a turkey, pre-stuffed with traditional chestnuts.

"Do you think we should get a goose now we've got one extra for lunch?" he says.

"No, we always have turkey. Even when Grandma was here, we had turkey."

"Yes, but she ate four mouthfuls and spent the rest of the afternoon drinking straight Dubonnet."

"Ooh!" I bounce on the spot. "We should get a bottle and have a little glass for her."

Nobody does butter like the French, creamy yellow and studded with salt flakes. I like it spread thickly on fresh baguette, but truthfully I could eat it on its own with a spoon. I add two blocks to the trolley along with cherry flavoured yoghurt, pots of grated carrot with Sicilian lemon juice, spicy *merguez* sausage, plump shrimp drenched in garlic butter.

In the soft drinks aisle I find my favourite Teisseire syrup in *menthe* for water, and *pamplemousse rose* for adding to gin.

"We might need a second trolley for the booze," Dad points out.

We don't need much from the bakery, thanks to the boulangerie in the village, but that doesn't stop me adding madeleines, *langue de chat* biscuits, and an enormous rosemary *fougasse* that I'll dip in olive oil and balsamic vinegar we have at home.

"Cameron seems nice, doesn't he?" Dad says while we browse the cereal aisle.

"Sure," I shrug, suddenly engrossed in a packet of pink sugary loops with a unicorn on the box.

"I think he's got a thing for you. Are you seeing anyone?" The question is as casual as if I'd like a coffee in the morning. We don't talk about this stuff, not since the last relationship ended so badly.

"Oh God, Dad, please stop."

"All I'm saying is, it wouldn't hurt you to have some fun once in a while."

"So what, I'm supposed to have a holiday romance with a man who doesn't live anywhere near me?"

"Yeah. He doesn't need to be your boyfriend. God knows you don't need that distraction." I press my lips together, not willing to tell him that since I discovered Cameron's audios, he's been a most welcome distraction. Every single night.

"This is so un-*Dad*-like. Aren't you supposed to warn me that boys are the devil and convince me to join a nunnery?"

We both laugh. Truthfully, he's never been that sort of Dad, the kind that opens the door with a baseball bat, but it's good to know he cares about my happiness.

We turn into the next aisle. "That's how me and your Mum got together, you know?"

"What are you talking about?"

"Holiday romance."

I spin around. "You never told me that."

"I was on a friend's stag do in Skegness. Got chatting to your mum at a rave, ditched my mates, and she moved in with me a few weeks later."

I am gobsmacked. I don't know which part of that story is weirdest, to be honest. "A rave?"

"Oh yeah, the nineties were something else, kid. I tell you what, though. You can have a holiday romance," he says, throwing the world's biggest bag of potato chips into the trolley. "But don't ever let me catch you at a rave."

Mac'n'Please

Rule Breaker

Wait.

Wait.

Hold it.

Look at you. So pretty when you're squirming.

You really want it. You're aching right now, aren't you?

Don't speak, just nod.

(Deep inhale)

You'll get what you need. What you deserve.

Chapter 22
Hannah

AFTER A DINNER OF cheese, charcuterie, accoutrements, and the fresh bread I picked up, we end up zoning out in front of some old James Bond movie Dad loves. I pass around the sugar cookies until the box is empty.

Cameron and Ryan are stretched out on the sofa, feet propped up on the wooden coffee table. I curl up in a ball in the nearby armchair, a cosy blanket draped over my lap.

I've only got half an eye on the film, scrolling through TikTok at the same time with one earbud in. I need the distraction so I don't keep glancing over at Cameron every thirty seconds. He looks delicious in a soft white t-shirt and his checked pyjama pants, his hair soft and fluffy after his post-ski shower.

Mum fusses over setting the table for tomorrow then snuggles by Dad's side, but it's not long before she starts snoring softly. Dad gives her a nudge, and she heads up to bed. He goes not long after, and James Bond shoots his way out of a building.

I'm practically begging the universe to send sleep vibes Ryan's way so he'll leave Cameron and I alone. Not that I expect much to happen, but at the very least, I'm hoping for a goodnight kiss.

I open our message history, wondering what I'd say to him if I felt bold enough.

Before I can start typing, a new message appears.

Cam: I wish you were sitting in my lap so I could kiss your neck.

I press my lips together and shift my body, blocking the view of my phone from the boys while I consider my reply.

Cam: You look so pretty when you blush.

Cam: I want your brother to get lost so I can get my hands on you.

This man!

"Who are you texting?" Ryan says, making me jump so hard my phone falls to the floor.

"Nobody," I say, bending to fetch it back.

"Nobody means somebody."

"It's my friend Rachel. From school." *There is no Rachel.*

"Better not be a boy."

Cameron's lips press together as he stifles a laugh and goes back to his phone. God forbid he gets the same level of interrogation as me.

Cam: Meet me in the kitchen.

"You want another drink?" Cameron asks, adjusting himself a little as he stands.

"I'm all good man," Ryan says. "I'm not pausing though. This movie is already way too long. Hurry, or you'll miss it."

"You want anything, Hannah?" he asks, the back of his hand ghosting over my shoulder as he passes by my chair.

"No, thank you," I reply, keeping my eyes trained on the television. *What do I do now?* How am I meant to come up with a fast excuse when I've sat here stuffing my face with cookies and wine for the past hour.

Looking around, I spy my almost empty water glass on the floor. I nudge it gently underneath the table and out of Ryan's view, then try to stand up and hold myself back from running to the kitchen. "I need water, actually."

I've barely stepped across the threshold when Cameron's hand darts out, closes around my wrist, tugging me out of view of the living room. My body spins into his and his arm loops around my waist, holding me there while his other hand finds its way into my hair. His lips crash down on mine before I can speak, and when he tugs at the nape of my neck, I open for him easily.

My hands find forearms and I slide them up to his shoulders, fisting at the fabric of his t-shirt. His tongue is warm, needy and searching, and thank God he's holding me up or I'd be a puddle at his feet.

"Had to taste you," he whispers into my mouth. "Couldn't stop thinking about it."

"Ryan is right out there," I whisper back while pulling him closer. I've never felt so torn in my life. He kisses me again, deep and all-consuming. I still can't wrap my head around it. Him, here, moaning as our bodies grapple to get closer than possible. I could do this forever.

"We should go back," he says, pulling away, eyes roaming my face as he fixes my hair, then wipes my bottom lip with the pad of his thumb. "You're so fucking hot, Hannah."

He presses a tiny kiss to my forehead, grabs his beer from the counter, and then he's gone.

I can't do it. There's no way I can sit in that room with my brother and it won't be obvious that I'm absolutely thrumming with need. I fill a glass of water, then splash a little on my face and neck. I'm sure it makes no difference at all.

Half an hour later, probably the longest half-hour of my life, I make my excuses and head upstairs, hoping Cam will follow.

Ryan stretches, yawning loudly. "I'm gonna head up too."

Oh, now you get the hint?

This is the entirely wrong combination of people leaving the room.

"I'm not fussed about the end of this movie, I've seen it before," says Cameron.

This isn't right either. I want the two of us alone, not all three of us heading our separate ways.

I climb the stairs with Ryan behind me, and Cameron returns our glasses to the kitchen, then follows behind him. In the hallway, Ryan is banging on about Christmas eve plans while Cameron throws me an apologetic look over his shoulder.

I use the shared bathroom first to wash up and brush my teeth, secretly hoping Cameron will come in and we can grab another moment alone here. My parents' room has an en-suite, but Ryan uses this bathroom too. It's still a risk.

Back in my room, I change into a baggy t-shirt and climb into bed, but I don't know how I'm supposed to sleep when I'm this pent up and horny. And is it any wonder, when all I can think about is Cameron lying in his bed on the other side of the wall?

I picture him with one arm propped behind his head, the other resting lazily on the crotch of his black and white checked pyjama bottoms with his covers pushed back. I wonder if he's stroking himself lazily through the material, or if he's slipping his hand inside the waistband for a more direct touch.

And I wonder if he's picturing me doing the same.

I don't want this to be how tonight ends, so I grab my phone from my nightstand to tell him to meet me downstairs. I'm about to hit send when my door slowly opens.

Chapter 23
Hannah

CAMERON SLIPS INSIDE AND closes my door quietly behind him. I sit up as he stalks towards the end of my bed and crawls up to me.

"What are you doing?" I whisper.

"Shhh," he says, one finger pressed to his lips.

He pulls his earbuds from his pocket, hands one to me, and pushes the other into his ear. I stare at it, until he gestures for me to copy him.

Fishing his phone from the other pocket, he fiddles around for a second and then I hear that unmistakable voice that turns me to mush.

'Can I tell you something?'

Through the earbud his voice is low and soft, but full of need. Here in the room, his hand settles on my knee, fingers dancing up to the hem of my t-shirt while he watches for my reaction.

*'I've been dying to get you alone again, so many things
I want to say to you... do to you.'*

I close my eyes and try to place this audio. He has so many, and they all start differently. I can't always remember right away, even though I know I've listened to everything he has posted multiple times over.

Cameron nudges my chin with his fingers and when I open my eyes, he points two of them back and forth between us. The message is clear. *Eyes on me.*

'Hannah, if I play with you, can you be quiet for me?'

I gasp, then press my lips together.

That's why I've never heard this before. Whatever I'm listening to now, he's recorded just for me, and now he's playing it back in both his ear and mine while sitting up in the middle of my bed. Cameron lays me gently back down against my pillows, then shifts to straddle my hips with his knees.

> *'I want you to listen carefully, sweetheart. I've been dying to touch you, and I can't go another night sleeping in that room next door knowing you're in here keeping this incredible body to yourself.'*

Holy fucking shit. His voice in my ears while he's here in the room with me is every fantasy I've ever had come to life.

'Is that OK?'

I nod gently, a willing accomplice in his silent plans.

'I want to kiss you for a bit. OK?'

He leans in and I'm smiling so much I can't even kiss him back.

'Your mouth is so pretty.'

His kisses are much slower than the frantic ones we've stolen over the past twenty-four hours. He takes his time, kissing along my jaw, darting his tongue out and flicking it over my lips, sucking my lower one deep into his mouth, then holding it between his teeth.

'I've been thinking about you non-stop. The way you kissed me back underneath the tree last night. I knew right then that kissing you wouldn't be enough.'

My hands grip his hair, those blessed locks that enchanted me the first time I saw him, while he works his mouth over my neck. Kissing, nibbling, sucking gently.

'I wish I could suck harder here. I want to leave you covered in marks so everyone knows who you belong to.'

The tension in my core tugs deeper. Possessive Mac does something extra special for me and he knows it, because I explained in great detail over DM months ago. All the embarrassment over that monumental fuck-up fades fast when I realise he can take full advantage of knowing what I like. I tip my head to watch him push my t-shirt up, hands coasting up my sides as he nudges it up just enough to reveal my breasts.

"Holy shit," he mouths for real as he drags his gaze over me. "So. Fucking. Hot."

'It's like your body was made for me to worship Hannah. I wish I could spend this entire night exploring you.'

Cameron's mouth moves to my nipples, his warm tongue sweeping them into stiff peaks.

'I've been wondering what you wear to bed. Do you wear underwear, or are you naked beneath your covers, just waiting, aching to be touched? If you're wearing anything at all, it has to go.'

He looks up, grinning as he shifts to hook his fingers into the waistband of my underwear and pulls them straight down my legs.

'It has to go because I need to see all of you. To taste all of you.'

This cannot be happening. I must be dreaming. Cameron takes his time, far too long, frankly, kissing his way up the inside of my thigh. I have to stop myself from pushing my hips up and straight into his face.

'Be patient, baby. You'll get what you need.'

How did he know I would be exactly like this? When he reaches the crease at the top of my thigh, I almost cry out at the feeling of his warm mouth on my smooth skin. He tastes and teases, swapping to the other side, skimming over the place where I need him the most.

'Watch me taste you, Hannah.'

He sticks out his tongue and sweeps it straight through me, a teasing lick that has his eyes rolling back. Heat blooms through me when he licks again, savouring, then devouring.

Past his shoulder I see his hips rocking against the bed and it turns me on even more to know how desperate he's feeling, too.

'Look at you, dirty girl, getting your needy pussy eaten. Ride my face, don't be shy, I can take it.'

Holy fuck! The sensation is unreal. His words flooding my brain in a way he'd never be able to while his mouth is solely focused on giving me pleasure. Cameron pulls back a little then pushes my legs wider, his thumbs spreading me open before he dives back in, the pressure coiling tighter.

'You're holding back on me, Hannah. I said ride my fucking tongue.'

My legs ache to push together, to clamp around his head, but he has them pinned hard and all I can do is squirm and thrust, fuck up against his hungry mouth.

'Are you aching to be filled up right now?'

My eyes widen, head flailing from side to side as I fist the sheets beside my hips.

'You have to be quiet. Hold your moan, baby.'

He raises an eyebrow along with his voice in my ear as my hands release their grip, both clamping over my mouth.

'I know it feels so good. You want to scream right?'

I nod hard. How I haven't made a noise yet is beyond me, not with the way he's licking and sucking, pulling my orgasm to the brink.

'But you can't. You have to be so good for me, baby.'

I am, I am, I am, I want to scream as my hips buck faster against his face.

'That's it, my good girl. You're doing so good. So good...but I think you need more, right?'

Cameron looks up at me, his lips glistening, watching for my approval. I hold myself up on my forearms to see him properly. He doesn't look away, but my eyes cast downward to watch as he circles me with one finger, spreading my wetness around before pushing into me and crooking upwards. My head falls back.

'Don't you dare look away from me now, Hannah.'

I snap my head up to watch him again. How? How the hell is he saying the precise things I need to hear in the moment?

Slowly, he adds another finger, and watches, wide-eyed and wanton, where they slip in and out of me.

He licks his lips, then sticks out his tongue again, the pointed tip circling my clit, flicking firmly against it while sparks fire behind my eyes.

The pressure not to scream is so intense it almost hurts. I grab the pillow from the other side of the bed and slam it over my face, biting hard into the stuffing. I don't care if I tear it.

My hips lift from the bed, but Cameron reaches underneath my thigh, looping one arm around my waist to pin me down while he fucks me with his hand. His lips purse around my clit, sucking with the perfect pressure to send that white heat shooting up my spine, down my legs, into my fingertips, my soul.

> *'Let me see how pretty you are when you come. Come for me, Hannah. Come. Come.'*

And I do. My need for release has been building all day, longer. Months. Everything tightens, then shatters as I fall apart for him, his hands on my skin, his mouth lapping me through it, his heavy breathing in my earbud.

A few seconds later, I feel him pulling the pillow away, and my arms down with it.

> *'Open your mouth, Hannah. Clean up the mess you made.'*

My mouth is open before I can even process what he's said, my core clenching at the absence of him as he looms over me, his fingers smearing a wet circle around my lips before stroking them over my tongue. Nobody has ever done this to me before and it's so fucking filthy. I love it.

I lap at them hungrily, sucking the wetness from his forefinger first, then his middle finger. When he pushes a third finger in between my lips, I realise why I feel so empty. He filled and stretched me while he took everything from me. I've never come like that in my life.

> *'That's my good fucking girl. I knew you'd be so hot when you come.'*

The audio ends, and he gently pulls my earbud free, tucking it back into the case alongside his. He places it on my bedside table and drops a kiss to my forehead, then another on my cheek.

We're done? We can't be done.

That can't be it. If I was home alone, I'd hit play immediately and listen on repeat for the rest of the day.

"More?" he whispers, ever so quietly against my ear, and I nod eagerly.

He takes my hand from where I've been gripping my pillow and guides it down to the front of his pyjamas so I can feel what all of this has done to him. He's thick and warm, a solid weight in my hand. I explore him through the soft material and watch his eyes drift closed.

He pulls a condom from his pocket and holds it between us, a silent question I answer with a soft *yes*, slipping my fingers into his waistband to help him undress. There's an empty yearning between my legs as I watch his cock spring free. I stroke my fingers down the sides of his stomach, through his soft curls, then wrap my fist around the base.

Judging by the expression on his face, he's having a pretty hard time keeping himself quiet, so I stroke firmly, payback for everything he just put me through. Not that I'm complaining. Only a fool would complain about the kind of orgasms that shift your entire soul out of alignment.

Sweeping my thumb through the bead of pre-cum at his swollen tip, I spread it around then bring it to my lips. How many nights have I spent dreaming of tasting him?

Cameron drops his head and kisses me gently, reaching down between us to replace my hand with his as he rolls the condom on and guides himself into me. There's no resistance, just an exquisite stretch and a sense of everything in the world settling into place.

His eyes flare and his mouth opens, so now it's my turn to keep him quiet. I press my palm to his mouth and he kisses it through a smile. He takes a second to let me adjust to the size of him, but then I'm rolling my hips, pushing up into him to spur him on.

He starts slowly, but every muscle screams as he builds, fucking me into euphoria. He shifts, flipping us over, taking me with him as he scoots up to sit against the headboard. My knees settle into the mattress on either side of his hips. Together we pull my t-shirt up and all the way off, his mouth seeking my aching nipples.

His hands reach behind me, cupping my ass and lifting me just enough that he can thrust up into me. My nails dig into his shoulders, my temple pressed against his as he pistons in and out. I focus on his breath, hot on my neck, as the pressure builds again.

Cameron drops me, and I squeak at the fullness, pausing before rocking back and forth, riding him as hard as I can, grinding desperately. His hands come up to grip either side of my face, angling it to one side so he can whisper up close. "I'm so close for you. Come on my dick, Hannah, I know you want to."

His hand drops between us, thumb finding my most sensitive spot at the place where our bodies meet. All it takes are two slippery strokes, the stretch of him filling me, and his words in my ear, for me to shatter again.

I lose control of my rhythm, but Cameron catches me, gripping my hips, pushing and pulling me as I ride out my orgasm on top of him. He presses his lips together, his eyes do the same, and then he's crying out my name on a silent scream as he thrusts, stills, flexes, and falls apart beneath me.

Beautiful.

Hot, gorgeous, sexy as hell, obviously, but beautiful, too. Cameron's face is lit up, chest rising and falling underneath my palms as he catches his breath. There's so much to say, but somehow we don't need to, even if we could.

Two years of aural foreplay have led to this moment, and I know now I'll never be the same.

I climb off, pull my t-shirt back on and roll to my side. Cameron deals with the condom then settles beside me, his arm reaching for the covers behind me to pull them over my rapidly cooling body.

"OK?" he mouths, and I nod. Better than OK.

"When did you record that?" I whisper as quietly as possible.

"This afternoon," he says back, his mouth close to my ear. "Your mom and Ryan were in the hot tub, so I didn't have long, I'm sorry. I had to whisper in case they came back inside."

"How can you be sorry? That's the hottest thing that's ever happened to me. The whispering made it even better."

"I wish I could stay here with you," he says, stroking my damp hair back from my face. I can only look up at him with longing for the impossible.

"Me too."

He peppers my face with tiny kisses. I want to fall asleep in this bliss, but he breaks the spell. "I should go."

"I'll come with you and go to the bathroom so it doesn't sound like someone leaves and doesn't come back."

We tread lightly along the hallway, opening the bathroom door and his door at the same time. We say our silent goodbye, hands reaching across the hallway for one final, electric touch.

Our festivities start with breakfast tomorrow, but I go to sleep feeling like I already got the best Christmas present of all time.

Chapter 24

Cameron

WAKING UP ALONE FEELS wrong. All I can think about is Hannah's warm body, in her warm bed. That's where I'm meant to be. Tucked in behind her where I can smell her shampoo and play with the waistband of her shorts.

I'm half-hard and I've barely opened my eyes, longing for her touch, the curve of her hips, that smooth swell of her beautiful tits. I thought last night might have been risky, but not only did it work, it ended up being the hottest thing I've ever done. Watching Hannah come for me, silently moaning to the words I knew would get her worked up. I want to do that again, all day, every day, but today is already working against me.

Apparently, Christmas Eve is the main event in France, and the Richmond family has a bunch of traditions they take part in. I'm unlikely to get Hannah to myself much today.

"Are we skiing this morning?" I ask, pouring my first coffee of the day.

Please say yes, so I can convince Hannah to stay behind with me.

I need some alone time with her like I need air.

"Oh no, my boy," Mark booms. "Today we feast. If your trousers aren't elasticated, you may want to change." He hooks his thumb into his waistband and stretches it out for emphasis.

"You've really caught the bug, huh?" Ryan says. I murmur my agreement as my eyes fall to his sister.

"Yeah, this place is pretty special." I don't add that my intentions aren't entirely pure.

"We could try to get a few runs in later," Hannah says, reading my mind. "But it's Christmas Eve, and there's a lot of other stuff you won't want to miss out on."

"Starting with breakfast," Cheryl calls over from the kitchen door. "Which is almost ready, so please get comfy. Mark, fetch the champagne."

I take the seat next to Hannah and give her knee a squeeze underneath the table while her dad ducks into the kitchen. If I could, I'd kiss her right here, and I hope she knows it.

Cheryl insisted we leave her alone to set the table last night, and it's quite the sight to behold. Stacked plates, crystal flutes, and multiple knives, forks, and spoons. Neatly rolled napkins in wooden rings painted with holly. Bowls of freshly sliced French bread, cream cheese, and pale yellow butter are at either end of the table, with sprigs of real holly scattered between them. It's fancy, but homely and, like so many times on this trip, I'm struck by a feeling of belonging. Something I haven't felt in a long time.

"Let the feast begin!" Cheryl says, appearing with a long wooden platter held aloft. Mark pops the cork on the fizz and Cheryl sets the board down in the middle of the table. It's piled high with smoked salmon scattered with fresh chives, wedges of lemon tucked into the pink folds. She returns to the kitchen, reappearing with a hot pan of perfectly scrambled eggs.

She takes off her apron and flings it into the kitchen before taking her seat. "Right. Tuck in then."

Beside me, Hannah stands to snap a bird's-eye photo of our meal, then sits and gestures for me to dig in. "Guests first."

"This looks incredible, Cheryl. Thank you so much."

"It's my pleasure, darling. You've really picked the best time to come and stay with us. We love eating."

"I feel like I should have dressed up."

"Oh no," Hannah says, shaking her head. "Save that for dinner."

"Um, I didn't bring anything fancy with me."

"No top hat and tails?" she says, cocking her head to one side.

"You're testing me, right?"

"I am. Don't worry, wear whatever you like."

"The French call this *Le Réveillon de Noël*," Cheryl informs me. "It's tradition to have a long family meal in the evening. We just like to make it more of a day long experience."

Mark pours the sparkling wine into our glasses as I help myself to salmon. "Is this your first Christmas away from home, son?"

"Sure is, Sir. Only my second time out of the US, actually."

"What's Christmas like in California?" Cheryl asks. "Ryan said he missed the snow when he couldn't join us."

"It's a strange experience. All the movies and books we grow up with show Christmas like this." I point my thumb over my shoulder toward the window behind me. "Snow everywhere, families having fun together, enormous trees, piles of presents. December is still pretty warm where we are on the west coast, so it's sometimes hard to feel like we're having a proper Christmas, you know? We give it a good shot, though. Everywhere is lit up, we have markets, and there's the Hollywood Parade down Hollywood Boulevard."

"I went last year with some folks from work," Ryan says, swallowing his food. "It was insane."

"Yeah, it's a huge deal. Santa is there with a band and dancers, and they have all these floats they walk down, like cartoon characters in elf hats and stuff. It's really commercial though, not much Christmas spirit."

"What about Christmas day? Does your family have any traditions?" Cheryl asks as I smear cream cheese on my bread.

"My parents are both dentists, so one is always on call and has to leave and deal with some emergency. Usually someone who'd had their teeth knocked out in a family argument. We'd mostly spend Christmas at my mom's sister's place. They had four girls, and they were spoiled little shits," I cough into my hand, "Pardon my French. They'd always wanted more toys, would fight over who had the best stuff. So much screaming. And they loved playing pranks on me, so Christmas wasn't much of a time to relax."

"That sounds horrible," Hannah says sincerely, her hand coming to a rest on my upper arm. I feel the warmth of her fingers through my hoodie, and there's that spark again. Always these goddamn sparks with her.

She gives it a squeeze then pulls away slowly, like she hasn't just touched me in front of her whole family.

Chapter 25

Cameron

AFTER BREAKFAST, CHERYL AND Mark busy themselves with preparation for the next meal while Hannah, Ryan and I head for the hot tub with more champagne in plastic tumblers.

It's less sunny today, the sky moody with snow clouds keeping the top of the mountain from view. The air is chilly, a light sprinkling of snow falling around us, though we're well protected underneath the canopy that covers the hot tub and the balcony.

"I need to pace myself or I'll pass out before noon," Hannah says when Mark appears to offer us a top up. All I can think about is how good it would feel to get naked with her and take an afternoon nap. To wake up sleepy and handsy. To inhale the scent of her skin from her neck while she backs her ass up against me.

Someday.

Sitting here opposite her is torture. With only the thin straps of her bikini visible above the water, it's easy to imagine her naked, and I don't want to get a boner while her brother sits between us telling some story about a job he's starting in the new year. I tip my head back against the headrest and close my eyes, trying to think about anything other than how good it would feel to have her riding me here.

"Anyone for sauna?" Hannah suggests after a while.

"Sure, let's go," Ryan says.

No, not you, man. Fuck off for five minutes.

Hannah wraps herself in a towel, a crime, as she climbs out, and we follow her through the boot room door to the sauna on the other side. Two benches line either side of the narrow room, with a third elevated at the back. Ryan and I sit opposite each other while Hannah pours more water on the coals and hops up top. I force myself not to look at her ass as she passes by. She rests her back against the wall opposite me, long legs stretched out in front of her. I can feel her eyes on me as we sit in silence, and it takes all my willpower not to stare back.

"What's Kayla doing today?" I ask, hoping Ryan has plans that get him out of our hair at some point.

"She's with her family this morning. We'll probably catch up with her at the parade later."

"Parade?"

"You didn't tell him about the parade?" Hannah gasps.

"I thought it would be a delightful surprise," he laughs. I look back and forth between them, confused at what events are about to unfold. "Trust me, bro, it's better than Hollywood."

The air in here is stifling, hot from the sauna, but also thick with tension and need. I feel sweat dripping down my back and my chest and I take slow, deep breaths to push through the resistance to duck out.

"OK, I'm done." Ryan says, wiping his forehead with the back of his hand. "You coming out?"

"I could do a little longer," I rush out.

"I'm good for now," Hannah agrees.

Fuck, yes.

And also, fuck no. As if the only time I'm going to get her to myself is in a boiling hot cupboard under the stairs.

Beads of sweat trickle down her chest. I follow their path with my eyes and wait a minute for Ryan to leave before breaking the silence. "Your bikini is driving me fucking nuts."

"I thought you might like it." Her eyes lock with mine as she pushes her breasts out and leans back, palms flat against the wood.

"You wear that to torture me?"

"Maybe," she shrugs.

"Consider me well and truly tortured."

"Show me your cock."

"Hannah Richmond. You naughty fucking girl." I push the waistband of my swim shorts down, revealing myself to her, now fully erect.

Hannah hops down from the top bench, perches opposite me, then bends forward to take a lick from root to tip, lapping at the moisture there.

"Yum," she says, leaning back and licking her lips.

So much for being shy.

I glance towards the door, an inconvenient panel of dark glass that doesn't afford us as much privacy as I'd like. "Show me your pussy."

She lifts her feet up, resting them on the bench as she spreads her legs and pulls the thin scrap of material to one side. Her other hand pulls a triangle of her bikini top down, revealing a hard pink bud that's begging for my mouth. What a fucking sight.

"Put a finger in," I whisper, and the sauna coals sizzle when she follows my orders.

"Oh God, I'm so horny," she moans, hips bucking up from the bench and onto her hand. I could watch her do this for hours, a private show just for me. It wouldn't take long until she'd be begging me to touch her, but I wouldn't give in so easily. Wouldn't let her come either, just make her keep herself on the edge until she was a squirmy dripping mess.

"Let me taste you."

Her eyes widen, and she sets her feet down and bends towards me. She reaches her hand out and I open my mouth to suck her fingers, but she keeps her distance, like she knows getting too close is a dangerous game to play with me.

I lunge forward, fisting the side of her bikini bottoms to pull her into my lap. Holding my dick against her, she grinds a little, making me slick with her wetness. Her head drops to my shoulder and I could punch right through a wall when she licks the sweat, bites into my skin, and groans.

"You can't fuck me in here," she whines, so precious and needy, rubbing herself harder against me. "As much as I want to, we'll probably get caught. And possibly die from heat exhaustion."

"Can you sneak into the shower upstairs with me?"

Her teeth worry at her lip while she mulls it over. "I don't think so. What if Mum or Dad call me to help with something? It's too risky."

"OK, well, I can't live with a boner this painful, so here's what we're going to do. I'll be in the shower, and I'll be thinking of you while I take care of this," I thrust up and make her squeal. "You go to your room and take care of yourself, but promise you'll pretend your fingers are mine."

"Promise," she says, moving to climb off my lap.

"Wait," I pull her back, one hand on the back of her head, guiding her perfect mouth to mine for a kiss that won't last nearly long enough.

Mac'n'Please

Bumping into your Ex

Of course I remember what you like. How could I forget?

I know you. I fucking know you.

Let me take care of you.

That's it, baby. Let go for me.

I don't give a shit who hears you come with my name on your lips.

(Panting and moaning)

Why did we ever stop doing this?

Chapter 26
Cameron

WHEN THE SUN GOES down, we bundle up in hats, scarves, and coats for the annual walk down to the village. Strings of lights hang high between buildings, twinkling decorations in the shape of snowflakes, bells, and candles everywhere you look.

Many houses have nativity scenes in their front gardens and though they're all similar, Cheryl makes us stop to admire each one. It's kind of nice to take it slow rather than rush through the day.

In the village, shop windows are lit up too, each fitted out with different displays. Hannah's face lights up as she guides me from window to window, pointing out things she's loved since she was a child. The streets are closed to traffic with stalls on either side selling fresh crepes, hot chocolate, and mulled wine. I feel like I'm in a Christmas movie.

"*Marrons chauds! Marrons chauds!*" a man in a fleece-lined hunting cap calls out, and Hannah loops her arm through mine to lead me towards him.

"*Deux, s'il vous plaît,*" she says, fishing a note out of her pocket. She exchanges it for two cups of suspicious looking brown lumps.

"What are you about to make me eat?" I ask once we're out of earshot.

"Roast chestnuts," she smiles, popping one in her mouth.

"Like in the song? I didn't think they were a real thing."

"Yep. Real thing, and much tastier than they look." I take her word for it, but am pleasantly surprised when I try one. Buttery and sweet, with a hint of rosemary and salt.

We pass them around as we follow her parents down towards the village square, passing the snowy slopes surrounding the base station, all lit up in pink and gold. Christmas music blares from the speakers as parents drag kids on sledges up and scream their way back down.

The square is packed with people, generations of families out together, wrapped up warmly in scarves and bobble hats. Ryan finds Kayla in the crowd, and everyone makes room for children to come forward for the best view. A chorus of *'Joyeux Noël'* and *'Bonnes Fêtes'* rings out as we pass people, and since the Richmonds say it back to everyone, I do too.

"Your French accent is good," Hannah says.

"Maybe I should give that a try sometime," I reply quietly, for her ears only. "A French lover audio."

"It would never beat your natural voice." She smiles up at me, and I want to kiss her so much. I don't know if it's her, or the overdose of festive cheer, or our warm breath hanging in the cold air between us, but this feels like a moment.

I should be able to hold her hand whenever I like, stroke her cheek and tell her what she's doing to me. I should be able to wrap a protective arm around her shoulder, hold her close to my chest, and rest my chin on the top of her head while she watches the parade.

I can't look away, and neither can she, until sleigh bells ring out and the crowd sends up a cheer around us, pressing us all closer together.

"He's here!" she beams, grabbing Ryan on her other side and jumping up and down. Whatever is going on between us, I can tell that *this* is the moment that means everything to her. Further along the street, a wooden sleigh on the back of a not so authentic flatbed truck, inches towards us.

"*Joyeux Noël, Joyeux Noël,*" the bearded fellow in a thick maroon robe cries out. He waves to both sides of the street, an army of elves in hats with bells on the end walking alongside him. Working quickly, they drop candy in shiny wrappers into the outstretched palms of children and adults alike. In every direction there are happy, smiling faces, and I finally know what it means to experience a real Christmas. Not one sponsored by giant corporations, one where everyone is present in the moment, and all they need is each other.

I quietly slip my gloved hand into Hannah's, and she leans into my side, discreet in the throng of people. This is how it should be. Me and my girl.

On my other side, Cheryl grabs my arm, and I begrudgingly drop Hannah's hand before anyone notices. "As the story goes, this is his last stop before he flies off to deliver presents on the other side of the world. Ryan and Hannah have cousins out in New Zealand, so they were very jealous he would visit them first."

"I think we said that one time, Mum," Hannah says. "You make out like we were always complaining."

"Oh, I know. You were good kids, but I thought it was cute," she chuckles softly, but it turns into a little sort of sob and when I look down at her, she's wiping away a tear.

"You OK, love?" Mark asks, wrapping an arm around her. She nods, sniffing as she composes herself and leans into his hug.

"I'm just so happy we're all here together. Quick, get a photo of me and the kids when he goes past."

Mark and I step back to make enough room for Hannah and Ryan to stand on either side of their mom, waiting for the moment the elevated sleigh appears in shot.

"Cameron, Kayla, you get in here too," Cheryl says, waving us towards her.

When Mark shows us the photo afterwards, my hand is on Hannah's shoulder, looking right where it belongs.

"That's a framer for sure," he says, patting me on the back.

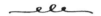

Dinner is a sumptuous, buzzy affair, soundtracked with laughter, clinked glasses and *'bon appétit'*. After another seafood course of buttery scallops and fresh pink langoustine, Mark fills the table with bronzed turkey, chestnut stuffing, garlicky greens, truffled mash and crisp sautéed potatoes.

"We couldn't possibly only have one sort of potatoes now, could we?" Mark says sarcastically as he carves the bird.

"The mash is my favourite," Hannah smiles. "But Ryan prefers the crispy ones."

"It's no contest," he says, biting down on one with a loud crunch.

"You can judge the winner," Cheryl says, one hand squeezing my shoulder.

"Oh thanks, no pressure," I laugh, spooning both onto my plate.

Mark and Cheryl embarrass Hannah and Ryan with stories from their childhood while we eat, and it's a beautiful thing to witness. A family whose love is abundant and inclusive, whose teasing is well-intentioned and never cruel.

My parents weren't even disappointed when I messaged to tell them I'd be travelling for the holidays and said they see me when I got back.

I make a mental note to video chat with them tomorrow, but for now my full attention wants to be here in this room, with these people.

After clearing the table together, we end up mostly horizontal in the living area, bellies full, hearts warm. The woodburner blazes, carols play on the speaker, and on the coffee table in the centre of the room we begin the traditional Richmond family jigsaw puzzle.

Time passes in a silent haze as we sort pieces into piles by colour, filling out the picture as we go. Mark snoozes in the armchair by the fire, and Hannah's socked foot finds its way into my lap underneath the table.

"Right, come up if you want *la bûche de Noël*," Cheryl says a while later, pushing up from the floor.

I know *Noël* means Christmas, but once again, I have no idea what I'm about to be served. It turns out it's a yule log, chocolate sponge cake shaped like a fallen tree limb, covered in ridged chocolate frosting, and a dusting of powdered sugar to complete the snowy effect.

"Wow, did you make this?" I ask.

"Oh, heavens no. Why would you bother when the *patisserie* make the best ones in the world? They add chestnuts to their recipe, which makes it extra nutty."

I burst out laughing.

"What's so funny?" Ryan says, pouring thick cream on top of his portion.

"I don't think I've ever eaten a chestnut in my life and I've had them three times today."

We're on the home stretch, pressing puzzle pieces into the last section while the fire crackles beside us. Heavy snow is falling outside the window, and I've had exactly the right amount of wine.

"Don't forget your shoes," Cheryl says, ruffling Ryan's hair as she and Mark head up to bed.

"Aren't we a little old for that now?" he laughs.

"Never too old for Christmas magic, my darlings. Sweet dreams." She blows us all kisses and climbs the stairs as we turn back to our puzzle.

"What's that about?"

"French children put their shoes in front of the fire on Christmas eve, so *Père Noël* can fill them with treats when he comes down the chimney at night," Hannah explains.

"That's cute. Do you do stockings too?"

She shakes her head. "Just shoes. We were always jealous of our friends back home who got stockings with presents, but it turned out they were jealous of our shoes full of chocolate too."

Ryan reaches for a bowl of nuts, throwing a few into his mouth. "When we were kids, Hannah would always flip out because my feet were bigger, so I got more candy than her."

"Candy," she laughs, throwing a cushion at his head. "You're so American now."

"That's it," he says, throwing it back. "I'm getting up early to steal your *candy*."

"Well, I got double last year because your lazy arse couldn't be bothered to come home. And the year before that." I love the way Hannah says *'arse'* in her fancy British accent.

"I'm throwing your shoes down the mountain so you won't get shit." He hops up and makes a beeline for the stairs that lead down to the boot room. Hannah bolts after him and a few minutes later they both come back, slightly out of breath, each holding a pair of their trainers. Hannah has an extra pair in her arms. Mine.

"Oh, that's... you don't have to do that," I say, hopping up to block her path. I reach out to take them from her, but she just looks up at me and smiles. That pretty smile that's throwing my world off its axis.

"Of course we do. You will not spend Christmas with us and be left out. And anyway..." she drops her voice to a whisper, "I happen to know Dad bought an alarming amount of sweets yesterday."

"Yeah dude," Ryan says, slapping me on the back. "You're part of the family now. An extra brother." Hannah raises her eyebrows in the exact same slightly horrified way I do. She crouches to line them up.

"There we go. Now all we have to do is go to sleep and hope Dad actually remembers to come down and fill them."

The three of us tidy up after ourselves and turn off the kitchen light before heading to our separate rooms. From the top of the stairs, I glance back at the scene below. A perfectly sized tree, not too tall to be obnoxious or too small to seem pathetic, draped in warm twinkling lights sitting in the corner. Our completed puzzle on the coffee table for Cheryl to admire in the morning. The fire is dying out and in front of it, three pairs of shoes wait for Christmas magic.

I'm struck with a vision of my future. My shoes, her shoes, and a bunch of little ones, all in a row.

Chapter 27

Hannah

CHRISTMAS DAY PASSES LIKE treacle. Chocolate from my shoe for breakfast. Elf on the TV. Leftovers. A dip in the hot tub. A nap on the sofa.

And Cameron.

Cameron's smiles across the room. Cameron's thigh pressed against mine underneath the table. Cameron's wink and a kiss blown my way when he walks backwards out of the room. Our little secrets.

I am in heaven, completely under his spell.

Yet we're never alone, and when it comes to the great Richmond book exchange, I feel terrible that I don't have a gift for him.

"In France, most families exchange presents on Christmas eve, but as we got older we decided it was ridiculous to ship a bunch of gifts out here only to take them home again," I explain. "So we buy each other books and swap them on Christmas Day."

Dad pipes up from behind his crossword puzzle. "You can never go wrong with a book."

"I'm really sorry. If I'd known you were coming, I'd have brought something for you, too."

"That's absolutely unnecessary," he says, pulling his phone from his pocket as he heads back upstairs. I don't blame him for wanting to skip out on this part of the day. My phone buzzes a few seconds later, just as he disappears from view.

Cam: You already gave me the best
gift possible x

Mum, Dad, and I pass our gifts around and I settle into the corner of the sofa to open mine. Of all our family traditions, I think this one is my favourite. The books I receive will be my closest companions for the rest of the trip, and my family always chooses well.

I'm pleasantly surprised to be given a collection of Nora Ephron essays.

"No law books?" I tease, reminding Dad of my first year of university when that's all he bought me.

"No sweetheart, I learned my lesson there."

"I have something for you all too, actually," Cameron says, dropping into the seat next to me with an armful of books wrapped in sheets of old newspaper.

"You do?"

"Yeah, your brother told me about your tradition, so I picked up a few things at the airport before we left."

"Cameron," Mum scolds. "You didn't have to do that. You're our guest! We didn't get you or Ryan anything."

"Trust me, it's the least I could do."

"Yeah sorry, I guess I'm outed as an airport gift purchaser too," Ryan laughs, producing his gifts from underneath the table. "And we couldn't find gift wrap anywhere in town, so we had to wrap them in *Le Monde*."

I watch as Dad opens a book about the history of the Hollywood Hills, and Mum a Stanley Tucci cookbook.

"Oh, my God. He's my celebrity crush," she shrieks, flipping through the pages.

"Ryan might have mentioned that."

Ryan's gift to me is a copy of *Anon Pls*, by real life Gossip Girl, DeuxMoi. "Everyone in LA loved it, apparently."

"And this one's for you," Cameron says. He looks at me for a second too long, then averts his eyes as he attempts to hand it over casually. "I hope you haven't read it already."

I open it carefully, unravelling the paper to find a copy of *The Twelve Loves of Christmas*, complete with the US cover. It's the perfect romance to get lost in over the next couple of days.

"You haven't read it?"

"No, but I've wanted to for ages. How did you know?"

"I took a guess. I think you'll like it, I was a fan."

"You've read it?"

"Oh yeah," he says, then forces his smile into a serious scowl. "For research."

"For research, sure. Thank you, Cameron." It feels like the most natural thing in the world to lean forward and hug him. His arms wrap tight around my torso and I breathe in the scent of him, warm and woodsy. My body softens against him, into a place where I belong. I'd go further, climb into his lap if my whole family weren't sitting staring at us.

Later, in bed, I'm engrossed in the book, exhausted and warm, half wondering if I'll get another late-night visit from Cameron. It's unlikely. I left him downstairs playing cards with Ryan and my parents, who all seem to have far more energy than I do.

It's all caught up with me. Work, skiing, the stress of sneaking around and keeping secrets with Cameron. We both know this thing we're doing can't last. Pretty soon we'll have to have a hideous conversation and bring this all to an end, but for now we're happy to play along.

Bone tired, I feel myself drifting off, but just after I turn my bedside lamp off, my phone screen lights up my room.

> **Cam:** I'm sorry I didn't get to kiss you properly today

> **Cam:** Can we ski tomorrow, just the two of us?

> **Hannah:** I'd like that a lot. We'll make up for it x

I fall asleep with my phone in my hand and a smile on my face.

Mac 'n' Please

At the Bar

You feel incredible.

Oh my god. What the fuck did I do to deserve this.

(Whimpering)

Can I come? Please?

Yeah? Keep doing that thing with your hips.

Oh, fuck. Yes.

Yes.

Please? Please?

Chapter 28

Cameron

HANNAH IS IN HER usual spot, stretched out on the chaise, book in one hand while the other rests a cup of coffee by her hip.

I watch her from where I've paused halfway down the stairs, wishing I could walk right over and scoop her into my arms. Her hair is pulled into a messy bun, just begging for my fingers to work it loose. Her mouth, currently pouting away at the book I bought her, belongs underneath mine. I feel that in my bones.

If I could just get five minutes alone with her, I'd make those the best five minutes of our lives. Then again, it's probably a good thing we always have company because five minutes would never be enough to satisfy the need I feel when I look at her.

"Morning, Hannah." I take the last few steps into the living area. "Where is everyone?"

"Morning Cameron," she says, her polite words overruled by her smile, bright and wide and all for me. "My parents just left. They're skiing over to see some friends in the next village. Ryan has yet to surface."

I stalk across the room and sit by her feet, dropping a kiss onto her bare knee. Her eyes flit to the stairs and I skate my fingertips up and down the soft skin of her ankle. "Ryan's with Kayla. He went to hers after you went to bed last night."

She sits up straight, dropping her book to the floor. "Are you saying we're alone right now?"

"I think so?"

She bolts to the bottom of the stairs. "*Ryan!* Are you up there?" A smile spreads across her face when there's no answer. "You mean to tell me I've been sitting here reading when I could have been sneaking into your bed?"

"I would have loved that. You waking me up with your pretty mouth." I hop into her spot, lean against the back, and pat my thigh. "Come here."

My girl is growing bolder, and wastes no time dropping one knee on either side of my hips so she can straddle my lap. Her hands find their way up underneath my t-shirt, nimble fingers skating over my stomach as she bites her lip and throws her head back.

My hands start at her knees, sliding up her thighs with my thumbs pushing up under the hem of her pyjama shorts. I want to take my time with her, but I don't know how long we have and I won't waste a second on conversation when it could be spent making her come.

Leaning forward, I tug her t-shirt aside so I can taste her collarbone while my other hand grabs her ass and pulls her further up to where my dick is hard and waiting in my pants.

She lands just right, grinding against the bulge. "Oh, Cam, please, I want—"

"Can I fuck you here?"

"Oh God, yes. Please," she gasps. I haven't even kissed her yet. I grip her jaw, tilting her face down and she opens for me, my tongue invading her mouth without a second thought, desperately seeking the bliss I've only ever found beneath her kisses.

I flip her to her back and press down on her hips, pinning her to the chair as I put some space between us. "Bend over the back of the chair and pull those pathetic excuse for shorts down. I want to see all of you."

She does as she's told, and fast. Everything blurs when she sticks her ass out towards me, plump pink skin glistening between her thighs. I want to eat her, tease her, or just sit and look. Admire every curve, every fold, every drop that trickles down her thigh while she waits for me to touch her. I'd love to get her begging, wriggling against nothing, frantic with anticipation.

Too many options and not enough time, but I'm a greedy man. I dip my head to lick from her clit to her entrance and back down again. Hannah groans and bucks wildly, hips pushing back against me.

"Wait right there."

"Where are you going?" Her voice is pleading, like she can't bear to be separated even for a moment. I can't pretend I don't love it.

"I'll be right back. Don't move a fucking muscle."

I take the stairs two at a time, rushing to my room to find a condom and hurrying back down. I kneel behind her, ripping it out of the packet, pushing my pyjama pants down past my hips and rolling it on.

"You ready baby?" She answers by wiggling back against me, arching up, hands gripping the back of the chaise.

I fist the base of my cock, sliding the head up and down her lips, tipping my hips to inch gently between them. She's tight, especially with her shorts keeping her thighs together, but she's so slick for me it only takes a few slow thrusts until I'm buried deep.

"Fuck. *Fuck!*" she cries out.

"For such a polite girl, you've got a dirty fucking mouth, Hannah." My words only encourage her, and she begins to send her hips back, matching my thrusts with her own pace.

I've been so focussed on her, the curve of her lower back, the swell of her ass, that I hadn't even looked up to remember where we are.

"Up straight," I tell her, pulling out and twisting her to one side. "Hands on the window."

Gripping her hips, I slide back into her and the force of my thrust pushes her up against the glass.

"Ahh, cold," she gasps.

"Good cold or bad cold?"

"Good. Don't stop. Never stop."

In the distance, dots of people weave their way down the hill and I thank my lucky stars their chalet doesn't have a neighbour in this direction.

"Look, Hannah. Look at all those people skiing past." She opens her eyes and I feel her clench. "Think they can see you getting your pussy filled up against the window?"

They're so far away they probably can't, but all Hannah can do is groan in response. "I can feel that, you know? You getting tighter on my dick. Dirty, dirty girl. You love this."

"Yes, yes. I love it."

"Lean back against me." She's so hot, I need to slow down or I'm going to embarrass myself soon. I pull her body to my chest by her shoulders and nudge her legs a little wider, keeping her impaled on my cock. One arm wraps around her front, squeezing her breast through her t-shirt, a perfect handful in my palm. The other strokes down over her stomach, seeking out the sensitive swollen bud between her legs.

A garbled moan escapes her throat, and she leans her head against my shoulder as I circle my fingers, spreading her wetness.

"So fucking hot hearing you when you don't have to hold back and be quiet." I press my open mouth to her neck, breathing into the tender skin there, feeling the vibration of her moans through her throat.

I find the right pace with my fingers, filling her deep, then rubbing her with slow, firm strokes before I pull back and do it all over again, a little faster each time. She whimpers every time I withdraw, her hands grasping for my wrist as I pull at her nipples, forehead nuzzling against my neck. She looks up at me, eyes wide, mouth gasping for air.

"Are you close, baby?" More whimpering. "You gonna come, Hannah? Right here on my cock with the world watching you?"

"Yes, Cam, fuck. Yes."

I keep thrusting and rubbing, sucking at the side of her neck, then moving to take her earlobe between my teeth. "That's it, my good girl. Right where I want you. Right where I own you."

That's all it takes to send her over the edge. Her moans give way to a roar as she grips my forearm tighter and trembles in my hold. I feel her clenching hard around me, the tightness of her thighs as her muscles spasm and shake. Her ass presses back against me, greedy, desperate to keep me deep until her orgasm subsides.

"Good girl," I whisper over and over, planting kisses on her temple as her breathing slows. My hand, still wet from her pussy, turns her cheek towards me. Her mouth finds mine, tongue seeking heat. That spark fires once more.

Home, my heart sings.

I could tell from everything she's told me so far that she has a praise kink, that she likes to submit. And as much as I love to control her, to push her and dominate her until she's a whimpering mess, right now there's something I need more.

I pull out slowly, careful not to lose the condom or send her crashing against the window. She looks over her shoulder at me, still panting, awaiting her next instruction.

"Upstairs. Now."

She tugs her shorts up from where they're bunched around her thighs and stands, catching herself on the mantelpiece as she wobbles on her way to the stairs. I should have carried her. I pull my pyjamas over my dick, catch up and keep her steady with my hands on her hips.

"My room." I guide her along the upstairs hallway, kicking the door closed behind us. Hannah spins in my arms, looping hers around my neck.

"Cameron, that was…" She doesn't need to finish the sentence. Not with me.

"I know, I know."

I walk her back to the edge of the bed with my arms tight around her waist and guide her gently down on top of the covers. "Want more. Need you. Crawl up."

She scrambles back quickly until her head hits my pillow.

"I don't know how long we have, but please know if I had it my way, this would be us for the rest of the day." I lift her t-shirt and press kisses to those perfect tits. All the way around her nipples, my tongue, heavy and flat on top of one, before sucking between my teeth. Hannah arches up into me.

"You're so sensitive," I moan around her flesh. "That's my fantasy. A whole day in bed with you to learn all your most sensitive spots."

"We definitely don't have all day," she argues. "Hurry."

"I want to take my time with you." I kiss down her belly, nibbling and tasting as I go until I settle on the bed between her feet. My fingertips hook into the waistband of her shorts, dragging them down and off before pushing my pyjamas down to my knees again. I catch her left ankle in my hand before it falls back to the bed and bring it to my mouth, sucking hard against the smooth skin there. I want to mark her some place nobody else will see.

"What's your favourite position?"

"I don't have one," she whispers, shaking her head, watching me with something like awe in her eyes. "Anything you do is amazing."

"I'm feeling pretty into this whole fucking with half our clothes still on thing."

Hannah laughs, this precious noise that could only come from a half-dressed woman on her back. I want to record it and play it back on a loop. Or better yet, hear it every day.

I am so fucked when it comes to this woman.

"You're right though, we might not have long, and I'm dying to be inside you again. Is that OK?"

"Yes, fuck, yes, please." She parts her legs eagerly. I move over her, guiding my cock until it notches just inside her. I drop my mouth to hers, swallowing her moan as I sink home, all the way in, right where I belong.

I want to savour this, savour the way she feels underneath me, her warmth, her skin, the way she smiles, lets it drop for half a second, then smiles again.

How is it possible I didn't even know she existed this time last week?

"Need you closer," she pleads, reaching under my arms to pull me down on top of her. I drop to my elbows and rest my chest against hers. My hips rock, my mouth never leaving hers as our bodies roll together, giving, taking, building up to that peak. Heat pools at the base of my spine, friction between us, tongues tangled, hands searching. Whispers and whimpers of *yes* and *more,* voices blending, breathing as one until over the edge we go. Together.

"I... Cameron..." she pants, her arms wrapping tighter around my back.

"I know. Me too." I whisper, mouth to her cheek, her breath warming mine.

I know, because this time it's different. This time it's magic. This time it's everything.

Chapter 29

Cameron

"Can I ask you a question?" Hannah asks when I return from the bathroom after cleaning myself up. She's still on my bed, her top pulled back down, but her shorts are still where I threw them on the floor.

"Shoot."

"How do you do all the sound effects in your audios?"

I flop down on the bed next to her and prop my head up on my hand. "Are you sure you want to pull back the curtain and ruin the magic?"

"Hmmm, good point."

"I'll tell you if you want to know." My thumb brushes soft strokes across her cheek.

"They're just so convincing. Like, way more realistic than some other voice actors."

"Well, that's because... wait, who else are you listening to other than me?"

"Er... are you sure *you* want to pull back the curtain and ruin the magic?" she teases, rolling into my side. "What I'm trying to say is... are they real? Did you record those sounds with other people?"

I can understand why she might think that. When I first started out, I skipped most sound effects, but as I got better at making audios, I realised they added something extra special. The sounds of skin slapping together, slurping, kissing, a little gagging here and there. They're hot noises.

"No, it's only ever me," I reassure her. "If you hear me masturbating, that's a ton of lube, everything else I had to get creative with. Most things are easier to replicate than you'd think. Except spanking. I've never managed to truly capture that noise without it sounding like clapping."

"Oh," she says, her head rearing back slightly. "Are you into that? I mean, I know you do it in some audios. I guess I'm interested to know what parts you really enjoy and which you do for your listeners."

"I'm not *not* into that. I never put something in an audio that I'm not into. Are you?"

"I don't know. I've never tried it." She bites her lip and I feel her curl inward slightly.

"Are you curious about it?"

"Maybe."

I roll to my front and shuffle my pyjamas down my thighs.

"Here you go. Hit me with your best shot."

"You're not serious?" she laughs, nervously.

"I am. I won't spank you unless you know what it's like to spank me first." I wiggle impatiently.

Hannah sits up and kneels beside me. "What's your safe word?"

I like that she knows enough to ask. She might be shy on the surface but I know she has a wild side underneath just waiting to come out.

"I like the red, amber, green system. And right now I'm all green."

She waits a few seconds, then gives me the most gentle of taps.

"Come on, you can do better than that."

She giggles, holding her hands up to her chest. "I'm worried I'll hurt you."

"Look, you know I do squats, I've got a nice juicy ass. You won't hurt me."

She raises her hand, and I watch as she brings it down a little harder, but not enough to make it sting.

"I don't know what I'm doing."

"You're overthinking it. Just open your palm nice and flat, raise your hand, and then spank upwards. So you get a nice jiggle." The *crack* fills the room, followed by her gasp, then mine. "Better. Again."

The next one stings a little as my skin heats up.

"Is that OK?"

"It's great, you're doing great. You can spank my thighs too, just not my lower back."

She goes again, firmer this time, and I don't know what's turning me on more, the sensation, or seeing her confidence grow before my eyes.

"Why is that so hot?" she whispers.

"I don't know how to explain it. But it's making me fucking hard again."

"You're all pink." She strokes softly over my ass, admiring her handiwork. "It's kind of beautiful."

"Do it again. See if you can leave a handprint."

My girl likes a challenge, and before I know it, she's reared back, smacked with all her might, then delivered a second blow immediately after. It feels fucking amazing and takes my breath away.

"Fuck, I'm so sorry," she says, smoothing her hand over it then dropping her head to kiss my tender flesh. I breathe through my gritted teeth as the sting subsides. "More?"

"Oh, you've got a taste for it now?" I roll to my side and pull her down to kiss me. "Maybe let's stop there, but you can let me know if you're ready for me to try with you. No pressure, OK?"

She nods, but the way her bottom lip catches on her teeth tells me I won't be waiting long.

I love how open she is, how responsive. My fingers find their way into her hair and I spend hours, minutes, seconds, I've no idea, stroking through the long strands that have fallen loose from her bun. Her eyes never leave mine, some unspoken conversation passing between us. Understanding, acceptance, love.

Fuck.

I love her.

This is insane. I just met her, but I know it's true. I've never felt this way before. I felt it the moment I laid eyes on her, and the feeling only deepens the longer we stare into each other's eyes.

"Anyone home?" we hear Ryan call up the stairs.

"Shit," I say, pulling my pants up fast and rolling to my front to hide the boner I definitely don't want him to see. Especially not since his sister is the sole cause of it. Hannah scrambles on the floor for her shorts, tugging them on, spinning circles as she starts to freak out.

"Hannah? Cameron?" Ryan shouts.

"There's nowhere to hide?" Hannah whispers.

"No, sit down here, trust me," I say, patting the bed and reaching for my phone on the nightstand.

"Helloooooo?"

"We're in here," I yell back.

"What are you guys up to?" Ryan says, throwing my door open seconds later.

"Just watching TikToks," I lie, quickly opening the app and jumping to my favourites. "I was about to show Hannah that guy with the chickens."

"Oh, that's classic, scoot up." I move barely an inch before Ryan vaults himself onto the bed, landing between Hannah and I.

Mac 'n' Please

Laundry Day

No, I wasn't expecting to get my dick sucked in the laundry room today. Were you expecting that? Or were you gonna jump the first guy who came in?

Hey, no judgement here! We all have needs.

You, what? You have a crush... on me?

Yeah, I've noticed you around. Kind of had a little thing for you, too.

Please, how could you know that? Are you a witch?

Listen, can I take you upstairs? I'm not the kind of guy
why doesn't return the favour.

I'm also not a guy who needs time to recover.

Leave the laundry, I'll come and grab it after.

Chapter 30
Hannah

CAMERON POSITIONS HIMSELF WITH one leg on either side of the picnic bench and pulls me in between his thighs, hooking both of my legs over his. I love the way he touches me, and I'm riding a high after our stolen time together yesterday. Though I could have done without the heart-attack caused by my brother nearly walking in on me spanking his best friend's backside until it turned bright red.

"I love this," he says, thumb brushing against the back of my neck.

"What?"

"This. Being here with you. This view. This pizza. I could do this every day and be happy."

"Oh, I'm glad I rank higher than the pizza," I laugh, taking another bite. He's not wrong though, it's cheesy and gooey, and exactly what I needed after a morning skiing.

"You taste better too," he says with a wink, and that low, swooping heat rushes through my body immediately. "I'm serious, though. I don't want this to end."

The heat turns prickly, the feelings I've been shoving down bubbling to the surface.

"It has to though," I sigh. "I don't live here. I'm going back to London and you're going back to L.A."

"I don't think I'm happy there." His confession bursts free so suddenly I think it shocks even him.

"What do you mean, you're not happy there?"

"I don't know, it's OK," he shrugs. "I mean, I don't hate it, but did you know this is only the second time I've been out of the US? I went to Mexico for a job a couple of years ago, but it was too quick to do anything, and I've been on a studio production ever since. I barely see daylight some days, you know?"

I hum gently, familiar with the feeling of working so hard you rarely take the time to step outside. Cameron reaches over to lace his fingers between mine, settling them together in my lap.

"Then being here, with this view, and this pizza, and this... you..." he presses a kiss to my temple. "Makes me remember there's a lot more to life than work."

"There really is. I'm so lucky I've been able to come here every year."

"I mean it though, you've shown me so many amazing things while we've been here. It's been unforgettable."

"It's been my pleasure."

"Your pleasure has been my favourite bit too," he growls against my ear before nipping it gently. I slump against him, my heart heavy knowing how much it will hurt to say goodbye next week. His free hand strokes up and down my back and I close my eyes, cherishing the peace I feel in his arms.

"I do pretty well from my audio stuff, you know?"

"So I gathered from your business class travels," I tease.

"I'd have time to make more content if I quit my job. And I can record those from anywhere in the world."

I jerk my head back to look at him. "What are you saying?"

"I guess I'm saying maybe I could come to London sometime? Spend a little more time with you."

Cameron in London. For me?

I couldn't let him do that. That's too much pressure. I wouldn't be worth his time.

"And what, make audios while I work? I don't even know your last name." I've been meaning to ask, but now, faced with the prospect of him travelling across the world to be closer to me, it seems urgently pressing to know.

"Don't tell me you wouldn't love to be a one woman audience with a front-row seat to the *Mac'n'Please* show." His fingers snake along my neck and underneath my hoodie until they find the soft skin at my collarbone. I bite my lip so hard I'm certain it leaves a mark. "That's what I thought. Dirty girl. Maybe I'll record while you're on a work call and see how long you can keep a straight face."

I'm woozy at the thought, softening into his body again. He's less careless with his touches now, and I don't seem to care about being seen with him anymore.

"Hmmm. Or maybe we could record something together," he whispers against the thin skin behind my ear. His breath is warm, and that low voice makes me shiver and ache between my thighs. But my body gives me away, tensing in his hold. "Oh, OK, maybe we won't do that then."

"I'm far too self-conscious," I admit, slightly shamefully. I'm pretty sure this man could get me to do anything he wanted, but the thought of him recording me twists my stomach.

"I promise I'll never make you do anything you don't want to do."

I tilt my head up towards him and kiss along his jaw. "Thank you."

"But I will do all the things you *do* want me to do. Just picture it. I can give you a massage after a long day. Bring you breakfast in bed."

That voice. It makes a shudder roll through me, and a tiny whimper falls from my lips.

"You OK?" he laughs.

"How is it that everything you say is so sexy? Or is it just that I've spent so long listening to your voice that any words turn me on?"

"Really?"

"Yes. That's how you're so good at what you do. You don't put on an accent. You're just you. It makes it so easy to tap into the fantasy that I..."

"That you what?"

I take a deep breath, drop my crust on my plate. "That I know you. That your words are just for me. That..."

He tilts my chin, angling my face up towards him. This close, his eyes dart back and forth and he tucks a loose lock of hair behind my ear. "That you're mine?"

"Yeah," I sigh. "That I'm yours."

The silence between us is a luxurious space. I feel the warmth of his breath against my cold cheek. He lowers his mouth for a barely there kiss as his fingers twist around my hair, tugging my head back.

"Naughton," he whispers.

"What?"

"My last name is Naughton. And I want to come and see you in London. Saying goodbye to you will suck. I want to give us a chance to see what this could be, OK?"

He believes in this. And his confidence makes me think maybe I could too.

"OK." I open for him, and let the anxiety slip away.

Chapter 31
Hannah

MUM IS FUSSING AROUND, tidying up bits from the day while we all hang out after a dinner cobbled together from the last of the leftovers. Ryan is stretched out on the sofa, while Cam and I sit on opposite armchairs, scrolling on our phones, occasionally sneaking glances at each other.

His knowing smiles light a fire low in my belly that doesn't take long to catch everywhere else. I want him so much, and I don't know when we'll be alone together again.

"For God's sake, Ryan."

"What did I do now?" Ryan says, lifting his head to look past me at Mum.

"Why is there a condom wrapper on the floor over here?"

My eyes snap to Cameron's as she holds it up for us all to see. His are wide, the colour draining from his face as he realises he must not have cleaned up properly the other day.

"That's not mine!" Ryan protests.

"Well, it's certainly not mine," she says, hands on her hips. "So whose is it, then?"

Cameron and I stare at each other so long the silence makes me want to throw up.

"It's mine..." we both say at the same time.

"What? Oh," Mum says, looking back and forth between us.

Ryan is sitting bolt upright now, shaking his head as he stands.

"Wait..." I shout, climbing out of my chair, but it's too late. He's already towering over Cam, finger pointing in his face.

"Did you have sex with my sister?"

Oh God, this can't be happening. "Ryan, wait, I can explain."

"I told you to leave her alone. Did you fuck her?"

"Ryan!" Mum scolds.

"Don't talk about her like that," Cameron says, standing to face off with my brother. Cameron has a couple of inches on Ryan, but the difference is nothing compared to their levels of anger right now. Cameron takes a deep breath, but Ryan looks ready to explode, snatching the front of Cam's hoodie in his fist.

"You used her? For fucking content?"

"Content? What are you on about?" Mum says and I have an out of body experience and start shrieking as a distraction.

"What is going on in here?" Dad appears from the kitchen, drying his hands on a tea-towel, but his questions matter least right now.

"No, man, no. It's not like that." Cameron holds his palms up in surrender. "I... I like her. I'm falling for her."

I hear myself gasp, fighting to get past Ryan, who pushes me back with his other arm.

"I'm sorry, Hannah," Cameron says, leaning to one side to catch my eye. "This shouldn't be the first time you hear that, and I'll say it again to you properly when I get the chance later."

I try to duck under Ryan's arm and Cameron reaches out for me.

"Don't you touch her," Ryan shouts, and then it all happens so fast. I'm pushed hard, tripping backwards over the coffee table, and Ryan is charging forward, knocking Cameron to his back on the floor. The thump of him landing, air whooshing from his chest makes me want to be sick, if the pain in my back wasn't searing through me already.

"Ryan, stop it!" Mum screams, rushing to my side. "Get off him."

The two of them are a tangle of limbs, twisting and grunting as Cameron tries to push Ryan off while Ryan struggles to keep him down.

"My...fucking...sister...you...dick," Ryan grunts out, throwing fists that never seem to land.

"Boys! That's enough," Dad shouts, pulling Ryan up by the back of his hoodie. As Cameron scrambles to his feet, Dad grabs him by neck too. I want to run to him, but I'm frozen to the spot, held in Mum's safe arms on the floor, both not quite believing the scene that just unfolded before us.

Dad opens the doors to the balcony and shoves them both outside into the chilly night air.

"I'm not wearing shoes!" Ryan protests.

"I don't give a shit. You're staying out there until you've calmed down."

My gaze falls to Cameron's feet. He's not wearing shoes either, just sports socks that cut off at the ankle. He'll freeze.

"Hannah," Dad says, crouching in front of me. His hands settle on my shoulders, forcing me to look away from Cameron and directly at him. "Did he make you do something you didn't want to do?"

"God, no. It was fully consensual, and I'm extremely mortified."

"So I don't need to kick him out? I don't care what time it is. I'll put him on the first plane home."

"No, please don't. I... ugh... I really like him, too."

"Oh my God, Hannah!" Mum's hands fly to her mouth. "Congratulations."

"What is happening?" I wince.

"This is wonderful. We're very happy for you."

"OK, calm down." You would think I'd just announced a proposal from this reaction. Do my parents really think so little of my love life?

Mum loops her arms around my shoulders and Dad wraps his arms around us both. "I told you he had a thing for you, sweetheart."

"You're not mad at me?" I manage to squeak out from between them.

Mum lets go and straightens up to standing, clearing her throat as she helps me to my feet. "We are never going to talk about whatever happened on that chair. But no, we're not mad at you for meeting someone who makes you happy."

"I'm going to get a drink and pretend tonight never happened," Dad says, heading for the fridge, and Mum sits down and goes back to her book. Out on the balcony, Cameron and my brother shiver, arms folded across their chests, shoulders up at their ears.

"Can we please let them back in now?"

Dad opens the door, which I now realise they could easily have opened themselves.

"You calmed down?" He asks Ryan, who pushes past him and storms off to his room.

Cameron rushes to my side, pushing my hair back from my face and pulling me into his arms. A small part of me feels awkward that he's touching me, hugging me in front of my parents, but it's overridden by relief. Relief that he's in from the cold, relief that our secret is out there. I hadn't realised how heavy it felt.

"Are you OK?" he asks.

"I'm fine. Are you?"

"If you're OK, I'm OK," he says, looking around the room like he also can't believe what just went down. "He won't let me apologise."

He sounds genuinely heartbroken, like a child who's broken a beloved vase, and knows they've done wrong but has no idea how to fix it.

"Here," I say, pushing one of the armchairs towards the wood-burner. "Take your socks off and sit by the fire. I'll fetch you some dry ones. Apologies can wait."

He drops into the chair like the weight of the world is on his shoulders, and I kiss the top of his head before going upstairs. Walking down the hallway, I pass my room, then Cam's, and knock on Ryan's door.

"Hey, can I come in?"

"Sure," he grunts.

I enter slowly and perch at the end of his bed. Ryan scoots up towards the headboard, wrapping his arms around his knees.

"Are you mad at me?"

"No. I'm fucking fuming at him, though. I specifically asked him not to hit on you."

"You can't ask people to do that. And it was a mutual thing."

"He does this though, Hannah. He..." I can practically see the cogs turning in his brain. "He sleeps with women and then he... It's not good."

"Ryan, it's OK. I know about Mac."

His head rears back. "He told you?"

"No, I... er... I actually already knew about his work. I recognised him the day you arrived."

"Oh, right." He softens a little, then tenses again when it all sinks in. "Oh my God, I don't want to think about what you're actually telling me right now."

"That's why I was so quiet when you first got here. I didn't want anyone to know, but he figured it out and then things just snowballed from there."

"Fuck," he says, raking his hands through his hair. "He's gonna use you, turn you into another one of his stories."

"Listen, I've been playing catch up here too, and I don't know how much you know about his work, but not all of those stories are real. They're just fantasies. He makes them up."

"No, he... he does things... he's into some kinky shit."

Lucky me.

I press my lips together and try not to laugh.

"So many women," he continues. "He'll only hurt you."

"I don't think it's that many, Ryan."

"You don't know."

"No, I don't know. So is he lying to me? You're his best friend, you tell me. How many women does he hook up with? I have no way of knowing. Is he bringing different women home every night of the week?"

"No, you're right, he doesn't do that. He's too busy working."

"He just has a good imagination," I say, memories of the way he tells stories rushing forward in my brain.

"Ew, stop thinking about it." Ryan kicks me with his foot. "Are you hurt? I didn't mean to push you."

"I'm fine. Listen, can you please keep this to yourself? I don't want Mum and Dad to know, and I don't think Cameron would either. It's mortifying enough that they know I've had sex, let alone in this house. I wouldn't survive a conversation with them about audio porn."

Ryan bursts out laughing. "Mum would have so many questions."

"Dad would want to hear some examples." We both stick our fingers in our mouths and pretend to throw up like we always have, laughing until the tension feels less awkward and heavy. I want to tell him Cameron is a good guy, and what I love about him, but I think it's best to avoid that subject while this all sinks in.

"What's going on with you and Kayla? Can I ask?"

"Same old shit," he says with a weary shrug. "She's here, I'm there. It never goes anywhere. It's not that serious."

I've never seen anything more serious than the way these two gravitate towards each other every time they're in the same location. "I don't think you're being honest with yourself. It's OK if you like her."

"What's the point if we're not in the same place? It'll be the same for you and Cam, you know? How's this gonna work when you're thousands of miles apart? How can he say he loves you? He just met you."

I sigh heavily and flop back against the covers. "Honestly? I have no idea. This is a very new thing that I didn't expect to blow up like this. I didn't know he felt that way about me. I think we have some talking to do ourselves."

"I don't want you to get hurt again," Ryan confesses, and I sit up, the past an unwelcome ghost in the room that we don't need to acknowledge out loud. He's the best big brother. Always looking out for me. "I don't think I will. Cameron isn't like him. Even if you're mad at him right now, you know he's a decent guy. And I know I deserve to have a little fun, even if it doesn't last."

"How did you get to be so wise?"

"Actually, those are Dad's words of wisdom. Oh, shit!" I jump up from the bed to leave. "I'm supposed to be getting him dry socks. Are we good?"

"Yeah, we're good."

Hovering by the door, I say my final piece. "Cameron would like to apologise to you."

He groans loudly and flops back onto the bed. "It's fine. He has nothing to apologise for."

"Then you need to apologise to him for trying to beat the shit out of him," I say. "Honestly, what were you thinking? That's not like you."

"I'm just looking out for my little sis. I'd kick anyone's ass who hurts you."

"Well, this is one battle you don't need to fight."

Ducking into Cameron's room, I can't help but smile at the memories we made in that bed while I grab him a fresh pair of socks. Back downstairs, I find him sitting at the table with Mum and Dad. I immediately regret leaving him alone with them, but then I see he has a mug of Dad's hot chocolate with whipped cream. Whatever conversation they've just had must have gone well. Dad doesn't make his special hot chocolate for just anyone.

I sit down beside him and hand him his socks, an unspoken thanks passing through us when he takes them from me, fingertips tracing my wrist.

Ryan trundles down the stairs a few minutes later, like a sulky teenager.

"You wanna go to Rico's?" he says.

"Sure, man. Thank you for the hot chocolate, Mr Richmond." Cameron finishes his drink and takes the empty mug through to the dishwasher, calling back as he goes. "I'll grab the sledges."

Ryan and I exchange a soft smile.

"You're coming too, sis."

Chapter 32

Cameron

RICO'S IS FULL OF folks rounding out their day on the hills, but a crowd leaves as we arrive, so Hannah heads for the bar, and Ryan and I grab a table. I'm grateful for a minute alone with him to clear the air.

"Listen man, I'm sorry I didn't tell you sooner. I never meant for you to find out like that."

"I don't want to talk about this in front of her," he says, checking over his shoulder and lowering his voice. "What the fuck are you playing at?"

"I should have been upfront with you, but I can't apologise for the way I feel. I didn't know she was going to be so... Hannah. She's incredible."

He clicks his tongue and shakes his head. "I'm her brother, you don't need to tell me what she's like. She doesn't need you coming along and screwing things up for her."

"I'm not going to, I swear. You know me better than that."

"Oh, you're not? What about when we go back to L.A. and she's heartbroken? I swore I'd never let anyone do that to her again."

"She told me about her exes."

"She did?"

"Yeah, she told me they cheated on her. I would never hurt her like that. Come on, man, I'm not that much of an asshole."

He drops his elbows on the table, raking his hands through his hair. "I can't get my head around it. The other women? She told me she already knew you from your work?"

"Yeah, I was pretty shocked at that, too. And I'm positive she doesn't want us talking about *that* either." I glance over his shoulder to keep an eye out for her. "As for the other women, that's not how any of it works. Bro, I've told you, if you have questions about my work, I'll answer them. Just not right now, she's coming back. Are we good?"

"I guess so," he shrugs, but I get the feeling I have a long way to go to smooth things over with him.

"Good, because your friendship means a lot to me, man. I don't want to lose you over this, but I won't lose her either."

Hannah looks gorgeous, ducking her way around a group of guys with a tray of beers in her hands. "Look who I found." Kayla tags behind her and drops four tequila shots onto the table.

"Let's celebrate you two finally being out in the open, shall we?" She hops up onto the barstool next to Ryan and slides shots towards each of us.

"You knew?" Ryan says, eyes wide, leaning away from her.

"Er yeah. Look at them," she says, jabbing her thumb at us across the table. "I knew the second I laid eyes on him they were hot for each other. God Ryan, you're such a dumbass. How did you not notice?"

"I must have been too busy looking at you." He grabs her stool, dragging it closer to his side. Kayla yelps, holding on tightly so she doesn't fall off.

"We thought we were being subtle," Hannah says, sniffing her tequila and gagging a little.

"Please, you were not. I saw you kissing on the slopes while I was teaching the other day. And holding hands at the parade."

Speaking of hands, Hannah's is much too far from mine, and I grab it, lifting it to press a kiss to her knuckles. Ryan grunts across from me and Hannah sighs heavily. "Stop that. We're both adults. We don't need your permission to do what we want."

"I just don't see this ending in anything but disaster. You live thousands of miles apart."

"Ryan, stop being such a little shit," Kayla says, smacking his thigh playfully. "Some people don't need to be together all the time. You should know that better than anyone."

"I like this girl," I say, pointing a finger in her direction. "She's smart."

"To long distance lovers," she cheers. She throws back her shot, and we do the same.

A few drinks, a few rounds of cards, and a lot of laughs later, things are feeling better. Lighter. Normal, even.

Hannah has migrated to my lap, and I hold her close, both arms around her waist, my thumb stroking gently at her hip as she and Kayla reminisce about friends that have come and gone over the years.

Kayla is a sweetheart. I can tell she's good for Ryan, and I feel like a shitty friend when I realise he's probably mad at me because he gets it. He knows all too well how rough it is to live far away from someone who means the world to you. He'd never mentioned her before this trip, but I can see there's something deep between them that can't be easy to ignore when they're apart.

Soon the bartender calls for last orders and we drink up.

"Are you coming back to mine?" Kayla says, booping Ryan on the nose.

"Yup," Ryan says, hopping off his stool to help her into her coat.

Outside, Kayla hugs us goodbye, Ryan gives me a fist bump, and then it's just me and my girl. She looks up at me, wiggling the two sledges in her hand. "Are you sure you want to do this again?"

"Last time led to the hottest kiss of my life, and I don't regret it one bit."

"You could have died," she says, punching her fist against my arm. "Promise you'll go slower this time."

"I was trying to go slow, then!" We walk arm in arm to the top of the piste that runs back to the village, and she shows me again how to position myself. We push off, and I swear I try to take it slower, but this sledge is extra slippy or something.

"Steer back towards me," she yells.

"I'm trying! You're too far away." I lean hard and start heading in her direction, but overcompensate, and the next thing I know, I've wiped her out. We tumble, rolling together for a bit until we lose our grip on each other and land a few yards apart with a thud.

My ribs hurt, but I push to my knees and scramble to her side. "Fuck, I'm sorry, are you OK?"

"Next time we're waiting for a cab," she laughs, spitting out a mouthful of snow, then rolling to her back to brush more out of her face.

"You're not hurt?"

"I'm fine. Did you hold on to your sledge?" Hers is still in her hand and I take it from her and jam it into the snow. Looking around for mine, I spot it not too far out of reach, but it can wait.

I crawl up over and rest my fists either side of her head, my knees at her hips. My perfect snow angel.

"So about that thing you said earlier," she says, staring up at me, moonlight reflected in her eyes.

"What thing?"

"The thing where you said you're falling for me." She presses her lips together.

"Oh, *that* thing." I smile and pull her up by the front of her jacket so I can snake my arm underneath her. "Any chance I can wipe that from your brain and you can act real happy and surprised when I say it again?"

"I don't think I can do that. Unless you didn't mean it?"

"Oh no, I definitely meant it. It's just... this is wild, right? We just met, and I'm feeling all these things I've never felt before. I'm lying in the snow halfway up a mountain and I'm falling so fucking hard for you, Hannah. I don't know how to explain it, maybe it's Christmas magic or something but I feel like you really see me."

"I do see you." She smiles that beautiful smile of hers, tugging off her gloves so she can cup both sides of my face. "I'm falling too, Cameron." She arches up to kiss the tip of my nose. "But I'm pretty sure I was falling from the first time I heard your voice."

"I know, baby."

"Because of the DMs?"

"Because of the DMs," I laugh, rolling to my back and pulling her on top of me.

She sighs, cold breath lingering between us. "Best stupid mistake I ever made."

"Those were so fucking hot, by the way. I don't know if I told you how much they turned me on when I read them." Her cheeks turn a shade pinker. My beautiful, shy, brilliant woman. "Don't get embarrassed. I need you to send a lot more messages like that once we get back home."

Mac 'n' Please

At the Bar

Do you... um... do you want to stay over? I could order some food, we could watch a movie or something.

Round two? Fuck. I'm so glad I worked up the courage to talk to you.

Of course I was nervous. Have you seen yourself? I watched you turn down at least five guys before I opened my dumb mouth to ask about your tattoo. Which is beautiful, by the way.

You're beautiful.

Yeah.

Chapter 33

Hannah

Five Months Later

LONDON IS SWELTERING THROUGH a late spring heatwave. I normally video chat with Cameron from the warmth of my bed, but the living room, with its wide windows, is the coolest place to hang out right now.

We've found a comfortable routine with me in London and him in L.A. Though we haven't been able to see each other in person yet, we haven't let a day go by without talking, even if it's just for a few minutes.

Most nights he calls when I'm home from work if he can grab a break from his shoot, or we speak first thing in the morning for me before he goes to bed. Weekends are my favourite. There's less pressure to get up, more time for him to whisper filth down the phone line, instruct me on exactly how he wants me to touch myself.

I'm not usually this nervous to talk to him, but this has not been a usual day, and this will not be one of our usual conversations.

I watch the clock on the wall tick over to 10 o'clock, then my phone buzzes and I answer on his first ring.

Ever so punctual, this man of mine.

"Hey baby," he smiles at me, as the call connects to a decent quality and his face comes into focus. "I have good news for you."

His hair is freshly washed before he goes to work, his waves finding their natural shape as they flop over his forehead. My face hurts from smiling when I look at him.

"I have news too," I say, biting at the side of my thumb.

"OK, you go first."

Oh, definitely not. My news is intense, high pressure, and will require discussion. I'm already halfway to a panic attack. What if he reacts badly? What if it's not what he wants? What if this is the end of us as a couple? We've barely begun.

"No you first," I insist.

He takes a deep breath, then pauses, before it all comes out in a rush. "I just heard I got a job on a new production that's shooting in London. As long as visas move fast, I can be there as early as next month."

"Oh my God," I say, my heart sinking faster by the second. "That's amazing."

"Right? I don't want to put any pressure on you. I'll get my own apartment, but being in the same city is something, right? I want to see you as much as you'll have me."

"Uh-huh." I nod, running options in my head.

"You don't look too happy about it," he says, and I see that furrow in his brow forming, the one I wish I could smooth out with my thumb when he's anxious. "Is this not a good thing?"

"It's a great thing, it's just—"

"Wait, what was your news?" he says.

"I requested a sabbatical to convert my legal qualifications so I can apply for a transfer. It got approved today."

"Oh, I didn't know that's a thing you wanted to do, but that's great news, babe." His face lights up on my phone, that beautiful smile that I'm about to destroy.

"The transfer would be to L.A."

I want to cry. He's moving to London, for me, and I'm all set to leave.

"Are you serious?"

"Yeah. I didn't want to tell you before anything got approved."

"Oh, holy shit. You did that for me?" I nod, and Cameron is silent for a second, before bursting out laughing.

"This isn't funny, Cam!" I flop back onto the sofa and throw an arm over my face.

"It's kind of hilarious, baby. Thank God we don't keep secrets from each other. Can you imagine? What if we tried to surprise each other, and I flew to you just as you flew to me?" He slumps down on his sofa, tears of laughter pooling in his eyes as his mind runs wild. "Oh! Imagine if our planes crossed over the Atlantic. Me knocking at your door in London, just as you knocked at mine in L.A. We're like something from a movie."

I roll my eyes at this daft romantic I've fallen deeply in love with. "You're such a writer. This is a disaster."

"OK, Hannah." He sits up straight, his tone serious. "What do you want to do? You decide this for us. I can ditch this gig. I'll go anywhere you want to be."

"I can't ask you to do that."

"Would you have looked for a job in the US if it wasn't for me?" he says.

"Probably not right now, but maybe eventually. There are some great opportunities and great clients out there. Would you have applied for something here?"

"Honestly, no," he sighs, and settles back against his sofa cushions. "And not because I don't want to do it, but because I hadn't even considered leaving L.A. until I met you. Now I'm itching to get out of here and see what the fuck the world has in store for me. I've never been to London, and I can't wait to visit. And you're the biggest part of it, but not the whole reason. I want to live a little."

He speaks as if I've brought out the best in him, when I feel he's brought me out of my shell, too. Maybe we've both given each other the push we needed in life.

"*Mac'n'Please* is doing well," he continues. "So after this sound gig I could get by on just that work, which means more time with you. We can take some trips, spend weekends with your parents."

I giggle at the thought. Cameron has seriously bonded with my parents, especially Mum. If he's not checking in with her and sending selfies from L.A., he's sending updates about Ryan, and telling her how much he misses me.

"You love London, right?"

"I really do." As excited as I was about gaining law experience abroad, I immediately started thinking about things I'd miss. The weird way we can have four seasons in one day, the iconic views as you walk along the river Thames, bacon naans for breakfast at Dishoom. I'd miss my parents and the few friends I've held onto. I'd miss feeling safe in my comfort zone. Cameron is the most bold thing to happen in my life, but he knows to take baby steps with me. Even the idea of starting a new life in L.A. where I know nobody and I'd get lost every day was enough to send me into a panic spiral.

"Can you ask to stay in London?" he suggests.

"Probably. I haven't signed anything yet."

"Then it's settled. Go and make the call or send an email or whatever. Tell them you're staying. And tell them your boyfriend's coming over so you'll be late to work some mornings because he wouldn't let you leave the house until you'd come all over his cock."

My eyes flare, and my thighs press together. He's always doing this, dropping absolute filth into the middle of our conversations. I can't say I hate it, and he definitely notices my reaction.

"Or maybe skip the last part if it's going to make your eyes glaze over like that. Damn, you really need to get off, don't you, baby?"

"Uh-huh," I moan, switching my phone to the opposite hand and pushing into my shorts where I'm already slick and ready. I circle my clit a few times with gentle pressure, forcing myself to hold back from where I need it most.

"Me too, baby. You wanna see how hard you've made me just from looking at your pretty face?"

"Yes, please." He doesn't need to be asked twice, angling his phone down to show me where he's gripping the base hard in his fist.

"Hey Hannah...?"

"Yes, Cameron?"

"Can I tell you something?"

"Please," I moan.

He talks me through my orgasm, his instructions driving me higher than I ever manage on my own. I watch as he strokes himself off, his eyes squeezing shut, mouth gasping as his release takes over. Afterwards, he cleans himself up, and I stay on the phone as I brush my teeth and head through to my bedroom. Then we lay, breathless and infatuated, on opposite sides of the world.

"Cam?" I whisper, sleep pulling me deeper into its clutches.

"Yes, my princess?"

"Will you move in with me? If you come here, I don't want you living anywhere else. I'll be working a lot. I want you to be here when I get home."

"That depends."

"On?"

"Does your apartment have good sound proofing?" he teases. "You're pretty loud when I make you come. I wouldn't want to upset my new neighbours."

Chapter 34

Cameron

Three Months Later

As far as *Mac'n'Please* subscribers are concerned, I'm in London for a year to travel, expand my horizons, and find inspiration for new audios.

What they don't know is that I'm living in a castle with my very own pretty English princess. OK, so it's a one-bedroom apartment on a side street, off another side street in Islington, but I sure feel like a prince walking these streets with my girl. *Popping out*, as the Brits say, for coffee and pastries on weekend mornings. Visiting museums and galleries. Bar hopping with her new work colleagues on Friday nights.

And as far as *those* people are concerned, I'm a freelance sound guy. I know Hannah isn't embarrassed about my work, but it's not always the easiest thing to explain to strangers.

We also decided, together, to keep our relationship private and offline, partly out of respect for the work, and for listeners who need to be able to tap into the fantasy that you exist only for them. Mostly out of respect for Hannah and our relationship. I'd never put her in an uncomfortable position, and the unfortunate reality is some fans can get a little obsessive. She should know, she was one once.

Although speaking of uncomfortable positions...

"Do you need another pillow, my love?"

"I'm good," she says, eyes closed, smiling softly. We've done this before, and she knows there is nothing to be nervous about. Only the location is different this time. My beautiful girlfriend is face down, head resting on her folded arms, naked on the soft blanket I've spread out over our dining table. A pillow under her hips has her perfect ass elevated slightly, and my microphone is positioned by her hip to capture everything I need.

"Red, amber, green, remember?"

"I know."

"Promise me you'll say amber if you need a break, and if you say red, we'll stop completely. Right away, no questions asked."

"I know."

"And you can't make any noise, baby." She nods and I smooth my hand over her hair, across her cheek and down to her mouth. She darts her tongue out, then whispers against my fingertips.

"I'll be good, I promise."

That mouth will be the death of me. My cock twitches behind my zipper, half hard at the sight of her and thickening fast.

If I've learned one thing about Hannah since we moved in together, it's that she loves to make promises during sex that she immediately breaks, consequences be damned. I would never have guessed that this rule follower would have such a bratty side, but boy am I glad I'm the one who brings it out in her.

I trace my fingers down the curve of her spine, smoothing over her lower back, then taking a handful of the ripe peach stuck in the air just for me. The anticipation is the thing that turns me on about spanking, knowing she has no idea when that first impact is coming. I like getting her all riled up and needy for me, and she's right there now, pushing her ass higher in the air, desperately seeking connection.

Leaning across her, I hit record, and keep stroking and smoothing until I snap my hand back and bring it down sharply.

"Fuck," she groans and hisses through her teeth.

"Do I need to gag you?" I growl low into her ear, loving the way she shudders and her eyes roll back in her head. She takes a deep breath and composes herself, shaking her head. "Good girl."

I stroke her more, her soft skin warming underneath my hand as it turns a little pink.

"Get ready," I warn her. I can easily edit myself out of the recording, but she holds her breath, bracing for my next move. I spank her a couple more times, with a solid impact that makes a satisfying noise and shows up nicely on my sound recording software. It's been impossible to get this level of accuracy on my own in the past. There's no substitute. When I tried to spank myself and record it, I ended up laughing on the floor at how ridiculous it was.

She looks so beautiful right now, her body a work of art laid out before me. This might start out professionally, and I need to nail this recording, but that doesn't mean I won't get to have a little fun with my girl, too.

"Remember, no noises." I keep my hands on her, dragging them down the back of her calf as I walk to the end of the table. Lifting her ankles, I spread her legs and set them back down gently, admiring my new view. She's aching to be touched, I can tell. Lips pink and glossy, throbbing, clenching around nothing underneath my gaze.

She brings me to my knees. I've got a job to do and I'm stuck here feeling like a predator who caught his first feast in weeks.

I spank her a few more times, and watch the way her body reacts. Her thighs tighten, and she breathes quietly through it, just like I taught her. I crouch down by her head so I'm in her line of vision, and stroke her hair the way she likes. "I need to do some quick ones back to back now, OK?"

She nods hungrily, and I'm so fucking proud of her. Of us. Of the way we bring out the best in each other. I had a curious mind long before I met Hannah, but with her I get to make all those fantasies a reality, make hers come true too, then curl my body around hers as she falls asleep in my arms. I'm the luckiest man on the planet.

"Three, two, one," I count her down, then *smack, smack, smack,* left, right, left again, then repeat it, up, down, down, up. Short, sharp slaps that build in intensity. Her back bows as she props herself up on her elbows, hands covering her mouth but still not making a sound.

She must be holding back so much. I wonder if she could come just from this. I think I could get her there, but she deserves more.

"We can stop there." I stroke the backs of her thighs, dropping kisses across her shoulder blades. "You did so good for me, baby. Well done."

She nods, lowering herself flat again, her face turned to one side. Her expression is hazy and relaxed, like she's blissed out from a deep tissue massage. Her hips rock as she wiggles her ass up and down and I'm not sure she even realises she's doing it.

Working quickly, I hit save on the recording, and move my equipment away from the table. From the bathroom, I grab a tube of Aloe Vera gel and squirt some into my palm.

Hannah sucks in a breath, then softens as I smear the cool gel over her, making sure I cover the tender spots where her skin is pink and blooming slightly.

"Cam?"

"What do you need, baby?"

"I need to come. Please? Please, can you make me come?"

"Keep those legs wide for me."

So many options. So many ways I could give her what she wants.

I pull a chair up to the end of the table, take a seat, and fist the blanket she's still lying on top of. Dragging it towards me, she shrieks as her body comes with it, sliding right up to where I'm waiting at the perfect height to feast on her. But not yet.

Swiping my fingers through her slick heat, I tease her with just the tips, little slow circles at her entrance. "Oh, Hannah, you're such a mess, sweetheart. What's got you so needy, baby?"

"You," she gasps.

"We'll have to do something about that then, won't we?" I stand, gripping her hips and pulling them up. "Get your knees up."

She scrambles to follow my orders, a dream bent over and spread out for me, but my patience is too thin for teasing anymore. I lick her once, twice, slowly, before diving in, lapping at her pussy, already overstimulated even though I've barely touched her. The sight of her fingertips gripping either side of the table is so fucking hot. I know I'll revisit it again and again in my head.

While she grinds against my tongue, I shove my pants past my hips, boxers too, desperate to get inside her.

I sit down and lift her into my lap, holding her legs apart so she can slide straight down onto my cock. She groans at the fullness, throwing her head back and I'm reminded once more how lucky I am we agreed to stick with her birth control over condoms. There's nothing hotter than being able to get inside her this fast.

"Ah fuck!" she yells when I bounce her up and down. "Ouch, ouch."

"Oh, shit, I'm so sorry. Do you want to stop?"

"No. No," she leans forward and rests her forearms on the table, giving her rosy ass cheeks a little space between us. "Just be careful. I'm a little sore."

"Sit all the way down and lean back against me." I pull my t-shirt up over my head and scoop her hair over the front of her shoulder, so there's nothing between us but skin and sweat. She sinks back, letting me take her weight. Pressing my thighs together, I settle her heels on the edge of the chair so her knees are up and open. "That feel OK, baby?"

"Yes." Her moans are feral and urging.

"Link your fingers together behind my head."

Now I have her right where I want her, exposed and hungry. I take my time exploring her body, stroking the inside of her arms, raking my fingernails along the backs of her thighs, pinching her nipples between my thumb and forefinger. Touching her everywhere but *there*.

"Cameron, move," she pleads, attempting to rock her hips but finding little traction in this position.

"Nope," I tease, sucking her earlobe between my teeth. "I wonder if you could come like this, just from squeezing around my cock and listening to my voice."

"I've come listening to your voice with less," she laughs.

"Yes you have, haven't you? All those months spent listening to me, wishing you could touch me, wishing I would make you come. No wonder you're such a desperate little slut." She clenches hard around me, the exact effect I knew my degrading words would have on her. "Can you feel that? Me throbbing inside you. Pulsing? I can feel you. Hot and tight and dripping all over me. I love it. I fucking love it."

She squeezes again. I can tell she's getting close, and I know I'm not far behind her.

"Are you gonna come for me, Hannah?"

"Uh-huh," she chokes out, her fingertips gripping the back of my neck. I hope they leave a mark. "Need... more..."

"Then get my fingers nice and wet." I push two into her mouth, and her hungry tongue soaks them, a string of saliva hanging between us when I reach down to finally give her what she needs.

She's already so slick, her clit so swollen with need, it takes barely any time at all to set her off. Wet circles, with just the pressure she likes. Her thighs snap together around my hand, but I keep stroking. My mouth sucks at the inside of her arm and when she explodes around me, that's all it takes to set me off, my cock pouring into her, hot and deep. "Oh fuck, Cam. Yes... fuck!"

I hold her steady as we ride it out together, kissing her neck softly, guiding her arms back down to her sides. "Good girl, my good girl."

Hannah's chest heaves as she catches her breath. When the aftershocks of her orgasm fade away, she drops her feet to the floor and I stand, carrying her with me into the bathroom. I turn on the water, pin her hair up with a claw clip, and help her into the shower. Careful not to put any pressure on her tender skin as I wash her body, I take my time exploring, soothing, worshipping. Afterwards, I dry her with a fluffy towel, guide her through to our bedroom, and help her slip underneath the covers.

"Mmm, that feels so nice." Knowing she'll be naked when I get into bed with her later is even nicer.

"I'm going to stay up and work for a bit, but I'll be back soon, OK?"

"Before you go," she says softly, reaching out to knit her fingers between mine. My other hand strokes through her hair, massaging her scalp, easing the tension I know she carries there. "Can I tell you something?"

"Mhmm?"

"I love you," she smiles, eyes floating closed as she nuzzles into her pillow.

"Can I tell you something?" I press a kiss to her cheek, resting my forehead against her temple as she drifts off. "I love you more."

Mac 'n' Please

Rule Breaker

It's OK, baby, you're OK.

I'm not going anywhere. Nowhere to be except here with you in my arms.

Just relax, sweetheart. Let me hold you.

You did so good. So good. I'm so proud of you.

Here, finish your water, and then you can fall asleep right here.

Just close your eyes, feel me stroking your hair, listen to the sound of my heartbeat.

buh-dum, buh-dum, buh-dum

Acknowledgements

As a holiday romance obsessive, I have loved writing *Can I Tell You Something?* and taking many trips in my mind to my beloved snowy Alps.

Skiing is my first love, and the mountains have such a special place in my heart. The setting for this book is not based on any one place, but rather the many resorts I've enjoyed with family and friends. The Marmot is sadly not real, but the French Onion Soup is, a little love letter to my friend Louise and one of the best meals we ever shared.

My first thanks must go to the many talented audio creators who selflessly put their heart and soul into their work. You are a true gift to the world, all year long.

A huge thanks to Gemma Flowers from The Lucky Type for your amazing work on this cover. You understood my vision so clearly and I can't wait to see this book out in the world.

Thank you to my beta readers Beth, Alex, Lauren, Becca, Bea, and Aoife for your early feedback and sense checking.

I have some of the sweetest ARC readers, the best hype team in the world. Thank you for making me feel even more excited about the release of this book.

My amazing Instagram community, thank you for sharing your best French supermarket purchases. I hope you enjoy spotting yourself in these pages.

The QCAP girlies, you are some of the funniest people I've ever met/not met yet. Thank you for spurring me on with links, gifs, reactions, and that screaming Pikachu face that I can't get enough of.

And thank you to Alex, for everything, always.

Also By Holly June Smith

Sunshine Book Club Series
The Best Book Boyfriend (Kara and Luke)
The Worst Guy Ever (Hattie and Rob)
The No Rules Roommate (Coming Spring 2024)

Standalone Romances
Just a Little Crush (Bec and Rennie)

The Best Book Boyfriend

**Who needs real-life love when you have a shelf of
perfect Book Boyfriends?**

Kara has sworn off men ever since The One dumped her without
warning. Instead she spends her evenings reading books with guaran-
teed happy endings, crushing on fictional heroes who'll never let her
down.

Luke is piecing his life back together after the death of his wife.
Opening Sunshine Coffee was the first step, but he has no idea where
to go from here.

When Kara stops by her new local coffee shop, Luke's clueless
comments about the romance novel she's reading are the opposite of
a Meet Cute. Determined to make a better impression, he asks for a
recommendation to change his mind.

Three books later, he can see the appeal. Who knew reading about
fictional people getting laid could teach you so much?

As their friendship blossoms into something more, their painful
pasts threaten to keep them apart. But if romance stories have taught
them anything, it's that there are many routes to love.

One road trip, a fake date, and a spicy readathon later, can Kara and Luke separate fact from fiction and find their very own Happy Ever After?

ele

Chapter 1 – Kara

"Get in here."

My best friend Megan grabs our other best friend Hattie by her coat and yanks her inside my front door. "You'll never believe what's happened."

"Someone's dead?"

"Grim. No."

"Well, I know for sure nobody here is pregnant. Hashtag dry spell. Do you know, I think I've conquered every single man in a 30-mile radius? There are simply no men left."

Hattie sets down two paper bags full of food and takes off her bobble hat, pale pink hair spilling out over her shoulders. She undoes her buttons while Megan, a Golden Retriever in human form, bounces up and down on the spot beside her.

"Hmmm. Judging by your reaction, I'm guessing... did a new Taylor album drop?"

Megan wiggles from head to toe and can't contain herself any longer. "Even better. Kara got a guy's phone number!"

Hattie flings her coat to the floor, kicking off her boots in different directions as she scrambles through to the living room where I am curled up in the armchair in my favourite pyjamas. I cover my face with my hands, a strange mix of excitement and embarrassment churning away in my stomach.

Hattie drops to her knees in front of me. "What? When? Where? How? *Who*?"

"Get the food and I'll tell you." She rushes back to the hallway, and I head through to the kitchen to pull warm plates from the oven.

Every Friday night for the past year, these two sweet angels have come over to hang out with me. Hattie brings takeaway, Megan brings wine, I stock up on ice cream and popcorn. We eat, drink, pull out the sofabed, and make a nest to watch rom-coms in until we fall asleep. It started out as something Megan called my 'Healing Plan', but now it's just our routine, and the highlight of my week.

It all started the night my boyfriend, well, ex-boyfriend, left me. Adam left me after twelve (yes, 12!) years.

We'd been together since we were sixteen and we had it all. Fantastic chemistry, good sex life, great jobs, beautiful house. Except while I naively thought we were heading for marriage, babies, dogs, the whole shebang, he was hiring an assistant who, let's just say, helped him spread more than just his sheets.

I can still picture it like it was yesterday. He broke the news while I was plating up dinner from our local Nepalese restaurant, here in the kitchen of the house we bought and renovated seven years ago.

There I was, chatting away about our upcoming holiday like a total mug, and he just stood there holding a suitcase he'd already packed. He said he'd met someone else, and he was moving out. He didn't even say sorry. I heard he took her on the holiday instead. From his mum. Can you imagine how devastating that was? Not to mention humiliating.

The night Adam left, Hattie and Megan were here within the hour, and they both held me while I sobbed my heart out. I tried calling him over and over until Megan wrenched my phone from my sweaty, shaky hands. After crying so hard I'd thrown up in the kitchen sink, Hattie forced me to eat roti while I wailed that I'd never be able to have a takeaway again.

"He's not ruining takeaway for you, babe," she'd said. "No man can ruin takeaway."

After making it their personal mission to reclaim takeaway as a symbol of feminism and friendship, here we still are. Even though I'd never admit it to them, I do still get a bit of a lump in my throat if we're having Nepalese, memories of that night still just under the surface of my skin.

"So spill it!" Megan says, filling three glasses of Sauvignon Blanc nearly to the top. "She told me when I arrived, but has refused to give me more details."

"There's not much to tell," I say, but they are impatient, crowding around me. I must admit I am rather enjoying having a story to share that isn't just about work for once. "I was having coffee in that new place in the old haberdashers, and this guy came over and asked what I was reading. We spoke for a while, then he asked me for a recommendation and gave me a note with his number on it. That's it."

"Just some random guy?" Megan asks.

"He works there." I carry our plates, cutlery and napkins through to the low coffee table. Megan plumps floor cushions for us to sit on while we eat.

"He works there? What is he 21?" Hattie says, clapping her hands together, throwing up a prayer. "Oh God, please say he is 21."

"I think he might actually be the owner. Maybe mid-thirties."

"What does he look like?"

"Brown hair, bit of a beard, glasses," I bite my lip to stop myself from grinning. "Checked shirt, nice strong arms." I can't deny it. He was hot.

"Oh, she's checked out the arms," Hattie laughs. "You're done for."

"I'm gonna die," Megan mock faints onto my sofa. "And he just struck up a conversation about books? He's a real life Book Boyfriend!"

"No, no. Don't get ahead of yourself. He was a bit rude, actually."

"Ugh, men!" they both groan.

After he left, my calls to Adam went straight to voicemail. He blocked me on social media. Deleted me from his life. No wonder I've sworn off human men. Instead, I spend my evenings with an array of exceptionally hot literary ones.

"Every week a new Book Boyfriend." The girls tease me about my obsession with romance novels, but I've found a lot of comfort between the pages of these sweet and spicy tales of unlucky yet feisty heroines and the charming, attentive men who are feral for them.

If there's one thing the past year has taught me, it's that my bed, a good book, and a small but powerful collection of sex toys is all a girl really needs. And I get through a lot more than one book a week.

I take a big gulp of wine and Hattie spoons egg fried rice and crispy chilli chicken onto all of our plates. Megan opens the prawn crackers and takes dainty little bites, while I prefer more of a shovelling it all at once in approach. "So then what happened?" Hattie asks.

"Then I left."

"*Without the note?*" she gasps

"No, not without the note."

"Where is the note?" Megan asks. "We need to see the note."

"In my book in the front pocket of my bag," I whisper, tilting my head towards the door. The two of them lock eyes across the table, then leap from the floor, racing each other down the hallway. Megan lets Hattie take her down in a fit of laughter. Her big heart always wants everyone to win. Hattie reappears in the doorway moments later, note in hand, eyes frantically scanning what I know is his very nice handwriting.

"Oh, Jesus," she groans. "Why didn't you start with his name?"

"What's his name?" Megan turns to ask me but I can't answer her. I pull my jumper up over my face to hide my blushes. "Oh no. It's not Adam, is it?" Hattie just stands there, mouth on the floor, fully agog as she reads it again.

"Kara! What is his name?" Megan is up on her knees now, both begging and towering over me. I just curl myself into a ball waiting for Hattie to say it, but she gives the honour to me.

"It's Luke," I whisper.

"Shut the fuck up!" We are all wide-eyed and shriek as if possessed. Megan does not swear, *ever*, though I can understand her excitement.

Luke Russo is the hero in *To Love and Protect*, an Italian bodyguard with a scorching body and a filthy mouth. Though the girls don't read as much romance as me, they do enjoy an occasional recommendation, and my love for Luke Russo had me shoving copies into their hands. We've spent many hours talking about him, his muscles, the way he takes control, all the things we'd let him do to us. To meet a real life Luke, well, I know where their heads are going right now.

"I want him! Read it to me!" Megan says, and Hattie clears her throat.

"He's written his phone number and, and I quote, *"I look forward to having the time of my life. Luke."*"

In seconds Megan is up and reading it over her shoulder, both looking back and forth between the note and me with faces full of joy. Hattie takes a deep breath as she sits back at the table and picks up her fork. "Kara, you're going to need to start from the beginning and tell us *everything*."

Printed in Great Britain
by Amazon